The Nine Thoughts

The Nine Thoughts

Stefan Kiesbye

Broken Tribe Press

The Nine Thoughts

Cover art by Stefan Kiesbye
Exterior design by Jacob Arms

Published by Broken Tribe Press
Lawrence Landing Company
Raleigh, North Carolina 27609
USA, North America

Broken Tribe Press is a proud member of:

Independent Book Publishers Association
 and
Community of Literary Magazines and Presses

www.brokentribepress.com

BROKEN TRIBE PRESS

FOR SANAZ

1

It took me days to enter her room. The note she'd left on the dining table remained in place; I taped it to where her plate would have sat. I didn't touch the dirty coffee mug she'd put on the kitchen counter before taking off. When I'd returned that evening after spending much of the day visiting with gallerists, only the dogs came to greet me. The patio door had been left open; they were hungry. Tonda had left a puddle of bile on the floor.

I texted Natalie before I saw the white piece of watercolor paper. After reading the note, I didn't text her again. I didn't try to call her. After reading her lines I understood that she would not pick up and talk things over. She didn't hate me — we'd lived together for twenty years without ever threatening to leave the other — but she had no use for me anymore. That morning she had watched me sleep and found that she could no longer remember who I was. She said she couldn't recall why she had loved my face, my body, or the way I spoke after I'd stirred awake. She didn't hate what she saw or heard, yet she couldn't make sense of my presence. She had outgrown me.

Things hurt more when you understand. Not even I could recognize who I had become. Most days I couldn't describe how I felt about living in this Northern California town, why I held on to work I had long lost interest in. I was comfortable, and on most days I would have said I was content, if anyone had asked. But at night I needed bourbon to fall asleep. I needed bourbon to stay asleep. Ours was a comfortable life, though when I thought back on the years we had spent in each other's presence, what stood out? What had we shared that wouldn't sound trivial?

Natalie who hated her name, Natalie who I'd never been allowed to see without make-up. My wife of twenty years who had never once said my first name aloud. Natalie whose lines hadn't changed, whose grace was as awkward as her conversation when among strangers. The wrinkles, the creases, the softening of her belly, had not distracted me. She had become more beautiful while I had been merely fading.

The trouble, I told myself, had started with the wildfire that burnt down our neighborhood, though it was a lie. Our troubles had started earlier, on days when we couldn't talk to each other over dinner. There had been weeks when neither of us touched the other. After our house and everything we owned had disappeared in the fire, we depended on each other, we grew close again. We drank a lot during the days of the rebuild. We lived on a ranch a few minutes from the coast and dealt with insurance and mortgage companies, with a contractor who declared bankruptcy when we didn't even have a garage door yet. Our love grew fierce once more. After we took possession of the house, we felt tired but hopeful, as though we were beginning a new life. Then the pandemic hit the following year, and everything ground to a halt. Every fall season we either had to evacuate or endure weeks of thick smoke, our air filters humming without pause. Somewhere in those years of the pandemic, we simply grew too tired to keep track of each other. We reminded each other of the worst.

*

After a week, her absence left burn marks on my skin. I understood that Natalie hadn't disappeared from my life because she wanted to join a commune in the South of France or India, but where had she gone? It's a funny thing — after first seeing her note I had accepted the finality of her decision. It was an epiphany that made me sit paralyzed at the dining table for over an hour, no matter how many times the dogs whined or nudged me. It all made sense. Yet shortly after, my mind began to spin its lies, its hopes, its small delusions, and on the eighth day after Natalie's departure, I sat down at her desk and logged into her computer. I wanted to find the guy she had left me for, the face of the man she had chosen to love instead of mine.

She hadn't changed her password in the past fifteen years. It had accompanied her from state to state and city to city like a charm. It had even survived the fire. What did I hope to find? While anger and vanity asked for evidence of an affair, I still trusted my wife more than my own feelings. And as though she had expected both anger and trust, she hadn't deleted the photos from her hard drive, hadn't bothered to empty her computer. It contained years' worth of us living the small life we'd called our own. Back then it had seemed charmed; people thought us happy. We thought so too. Doubt had crept in, though, and slowly grown bigger. I had sometimes watched Natalie cleaning the kitchen after dinner, listening to the radio or a podcast or her playlist on Spotify, and I had felt as though I wasn't even in the same room with her, as though I were a stranger and watching my wife through a window. I couldn't feel anything connecting us. Then she would turn, notice me staring, and smile or throw the kitchen towel at me before walking out onto the back patio and smoking weed.

In the first years of our marriage I sang to her. I improvised songs, improvised lyrics, and serenaded her in the shower or at the stove. She complained, maybe she was embarrassed or maybe annoyed, and I slowly stopped. Once in a long while I'd sing for her in the car, but she would look away or turn on the radio. I have a good baritone, I sang in choirs and bands for years, but my voice appeared to make her uneasy, as though I had turned into someone she didn't care to know. You know how sometimes you take a picture of someone you love but you catch them at a bad angle, in impossible light, and somehow you wish you hadn't taken that picture and can't unsee it? Whenever I started singing to her, Natalie must have seen me in such a way.

The photos on her computer were a disappointment at first. It was painful to watch us together, grinning for selfies that she'd stopped posting on Facebook or Instagram during the rebuild. But there was little I hadn't seen. A few photos of colleagues at the library, taken before we had moved back into our neighborhood and she had stopped working. Pictures of a holiday party, of Halloween costumes. Then I noticed small pockets of photos Natalie had taken of herself. More and more appeared as the months went on. She was trying on new clothes, new poses, as though she hadn't ever seen herself before and wanted to find out what that person looked like. They were carefully taken, though not staged, if that makes any sense. They didn't aspire to be art or even artsy, they were merely trying to take a close look at who this woman might be. They were looking for potential, hidden features, neglected sides. They were looking for beauty.

I gawked at that woman. She was more than I had seen in Natalie. I got so scared, I shut down the computer and mixed myself a drink. Whenever feelings threatened the careful invention of who I was and had become, shiny from wear in some spaces, intentionally out-of-focus elsewhere, I saw to the dogs' needs, rubbed ears, bellies, checked their fur for stickers. Anemone didn't much care for my affection, she might have smelled the need, the greediness, the dark spots in my mind I wanted to keep untouched, yet Tonda didn't care that my love was a distraction. He took it, ran with it, enjoyed it as much as the real thing.

*

Once your partner is gone, you notice how much of your life never fully belonged to you. I discovered silences, pockets of time left unfilled, spaces inside the house that now felt irrelevant, hostile even. The sounds of my wife determined to finish a task or talking to herself in her room were absent; I felt shunned by a bookshelf without a single title I'd picked or read. I couldn't remember ever using the blue loveseat, only ever sat on one of the four dining room chairs. No smell of food I hadn't cooked myself interrupted my days, no smell of coffee I hadn't prepared. Nobody urged me to start breakfast or switch on the news. No bits and pieces other than my own formed small islands on every table, every bench.

I told myself I would no longer try to find Natalie, and yet, a day later I started up her desktop again. A few photographs showed her friend Sonia in a park, at a restaurant, in the car next to Natalie, on a walk along the Russian River. I knew Sonia, but in recent years, she had turned from a mutual friend into Natalie's friend alone. I hadn't seen her in months. Sonia's husband Craig and I had met on the artisan market circuit, before his source of Moroccan chests had dried up and I bought a small gallery space to sell the large canvases I produced in my garage. He and Sonia still lived in Rohnert Park, a twenty-minute drive from our house, but I hadn't been able to keep up the friendship. I wasn't good at being friends. Love I understood, but friendship seemed so much more demanding.

Those were the last photos Natalie had taken. Pictures of herself and those of Sonia, but nothing seemed to hint at anything untoward. After another four hours, I had looked at the entire trove a second time.

One picture I had overlooked twice, and only paid attention to on the third try because Tonda nudged me. It was 4:00 pm, feeding time. The shot had been taken hastily — a photo of a poster or a brochure. It was slightly blurry, but when I enlarged it, I was able to read the text below the photo of a cottage and forested mountains. 'Retreat. Discover the healing powers of your body and soul. Let yourself be guided by healer Ursa Carmel.' If there was a number or an address on that poster or brochure, it had been cut off.

Seven hours after I had begun my second search, I ended it by sending Natalie's computer back to sleep. My eyes were burning, my vision had turned fuzzy around the edges. In the kitchen, I mixed myself a drink and went into the backyard, staring at my neighbor's camping trailer, his trees, the mountains beyond the 101. Then I called Sonia. She picked up after the first ring and sounded surprised, though not in an unpleasant way. Hers was the voice of a chipper high school teacher, always ready to entertain a rowdy crowd of teenagers, always ready to get stern without warning. I told her Natalie had left, and because my throat and mouth turned dry after those few words, I couldn't continue. She didn't make a sound. There was no "Oh, I'm sorry," no "How are you holding up?" We were both silent until I finally coughed and asked with a scratchy voice, "You knew she was going to leave me?"

There was more silence coming from Sonia's end. Then, "I had my suspicions. She was, she acted...she wasn't really herself." Sonia paused for a second. "That's not what I mean. Maybe she was..."

"More herself?"

"Perhaps. She was definitely different."

"Did she say where she was headed? What she was going to do?" I winced at my words. Those were words coming from a distant relative, some clueless investigator, not Natalie's husband of twenty years.

Still more silence followed.

"It's okay if you can't talk about it," I said. "I understand."

"It's not that," Sonia said. "But I just don't know." No longer did her words sound chipper; the high school voice had dissipated. Her next words were spoken with a flat affect. "I can't help you. I just can't."

Before she could end the call, I asked her about the brochure.

"Did she go see Ursa Carmel? Did you guys go together?"

"I really can't help you," she said. "It's impossible. Don't call again. Please."

Craig called about an hour after Sonia had hung up on me. His first words were, "Is she okay?"

I didn't answer immediately. There was a harshness to his voice I couldn't place or explain. "I haven't…I don't know where she is."

"You upset Sonia. She's besides herself. I can't get anything out of her."

"I just…"

"You should go to the police." He said this so brusquely I nearly had to laugh. Part of me wanted to punch him. We hadn't talked in months and now he was trying to give me advice?

"Why?" I asked as calmly as I could.

"You shouldn't hide her disappearance," he said, as though this were self-evident.

"She's left me a note. She's left me."

He didn't respond immediately, though I could hear, or thought I could hear, Craig sucking in air as if getting ready to speak, Craig exhaling in wordless exasperation. I might have imagined those sounds. I might have anticipated hearing them. He could be a self-righteous prick.

"It's none of my business, and I understand that I can't put myself in your shoes, but you need to contact the police. They need to know what happened. You should be frank."

"'What happened'? You tell me what happened."

This time his refusal to answer was more complete and lasted much longer. "I've got to go now," he finally said. "Sonia…" Then he hung up.

That night I took stock of my finances. Whatever Natalie and I had owned, one half was hers. When would she contact me to deal with the financial fallout of the end of our relationship? Would I be able to keep the house and buy her out? I looked at our shared account, at our investments, our private retirement plans. And an ugly thought crept into my worries, feeding on my shame, my dejection, the empty side of the bed we had shared for so many years — it would be more advantageous if she never contacted me at all and stayed disappeared.

*

Of course, I did what anyone in my situation would have done and searched the healer's name online. In college, my roommate's name had been Jim Turner, and after not staying in touch with him after graduation, it was now impossible to locate him. His name rendered him invisible. But I felt certain that Ursa Carmel would turn out to be unique.

It had the pungent smell of an adopted name, invented to suggest to possible clients an air of mystique and new age of the old-school kind. The kind where self-discovery still led to a harmonious universe and worldwide peace.

To my surprise, there were no hits. None whatsoever. The name didn't exist. I looked at the printout of the photo and no, I hadn't been mistaken. Ursa Carmel. How could a healer who advertised in brochures not be on the internet? How did she stay off Yelp?

Craig's call had disturbed me more than I cared to admit. What had Sonia told him? What allegations had she voiced? My wife had left me of her own free will. She had left without giving me a hint of her whereabouts. I had expected a bit of compassion and commiseration, not the anger directed at me by a former friend. Why should I have to approach the police? What crime had I committed? Natalie hadn't been abducted. She hadn't been kidnapped. What did the police have to do with anything?

Next, I checked Natalie's emails. We had never snooped on each other, had never read each other's notebooks. I had never touched her diary, nor had she ever combed through the letters and writings covering my desk. We had been safe in the knowledge that we respected each other's privacy. We trusted the other, we had never felt the need not to. What was hers was hers alone; I had not felt threatened by her thoughts or her dreams.

I never delete emails of any importance. My inbox is the history of my life. Natalie's, however, held less than a hundred messages. I felt certain that she hadn't taken the time to clean up and discard any possible traces — she merely hated clutter, always had.

The oldest message was from six or seven months prior, a receipt for an online purchase. She had kept two emails with our dogs' vaccination records, a few invitations to parties, and some messages from her parents who had recently moved to Arizona.

A month before she had left me, someone named Ben Miller had sent her a photo attachment. The picture was a selfie taken by who I supposed was Ben, a guy with a three-day shadow wearing a baseball cap and large sunglasses — he could have been anyone. Only the graying stubble and a slight slackening of his chin made me think that he had to be in his fifties or even sixties. Behind him appeared Natalie's head. She, too, was wearing a cap, but no sunglasses hid her eyes. She wasn't beaming exactly, but she seemed full of joy. Behind her I could make out the contours of the Sebastopol Public Library.

The message accompanying the photo was brief. "You're in," it read. Nothing more.

*

A year after the fires, during the first weeks of our rebuild, I started cleaning up Portuguese Beach north of Bodega Bay. This was the first beach Natalie and I had discovered with our dogs, and we had returned repeatedly to walk along its three sections divided by steep rock outcroppings. During high tide, you could only access them separately, but during low tide they connected, and to get from one end to the other and back took over an hour and a half.

Once a week I made the forty-five-minute drive and collected what other visitors had left behind or what the ocean had spit out onto the coarse sand. Pieces of styrofoam, filled poop bags, filled diapers, soda and hard-seltzer cans, tires, plastic bottles, beer bottles — mostly Modelo — kids' toys, food wrappers, fishing gear. I used these walks to diminish the anxiety of my days, to shrink my fears, to indulge in the childish joy of finding small, brightly colored kids' shovels or mud-pie forms. We depended on sales of my work, but I found little time to paint. The garage had doubled as my studio, and the small modular home we moved into offered no workspace. While demand for the large canvases was still high, every day spent at the construction site or on the phone with the contractor's office and the mortgage company made me question the choices I had made in my career. Life in California was so expensive, I couldn't afford to lose any sales. The mortgage on our house ate much of what my paintings brought in; any dip in income might mean having to move to another state.

But during the brief hours on the beach, the world of work and mortgages receded. The coastline was harsh, the cliffs raggedy and steep, and during rainy season, parts of Highway 1 fell into the ocean below. The beaches were pockets of another world, secluded, accessible only by slippery and badly maintained paths. The beaches didn't know who you were or what had destroyed your home. The beaches didn't remind you of anything.

The morning after I had found the selfie of my wife and her friend —
I didn't want to call him a lover yet; I resisted to speculate what he might
look like or where she might have met him — I left the dogs at home and
drove out to Bodega Bay. Santa Rosa had been sunny, but fog lingered
near the coastline. This was late June, a Saturday, and Friday night had
left the beach in disarray. Several somebodies had taken twenty-four
bottles of Corona and a tray of aluminum-wrapped food to picnic near
the cliff and discarded the bottles among the ice plants. A camping chair
had been abandoned at water's edge. A blanket and socks lay about.

I stuffed blanket and bottles and tissues and poop bags into my 18-
gallon bag and walked north in a zig-zagging line, trying to spot those
brightly colored somethings — wrappers, toys, soda cans — from afar.
After maybe fifteen minutes, my feet took over, guiding me without
thinking, focusing on just the tell-tale signs of half-buried trash. During
these walks I barely *looked* at the ocean. I didn't have to. It filled my ears
and nose, it splashed about my feet, and at times threatened to pin me to
a rock. The fog further isolated me from the traffic above and the houses
rented out to vacationers from San Francisco or San Jose. Much of the
cliffs disappeared from view. I couldn't feel my world, I was a mere body.

"You're in." What could Natalie's friend have meant? "You're in."
Had she applied for a job or some kind of membership? Or was this the
man's way of telling her how much he cared? Had she entered his heart
and mind? How could I have not been part of whatever it was she had
wanted to do? How could I have missed the signs that she was preparing
to leave? Why had my wife wanted me to miss the moment this man told
her, "You're in"?

Towards the end of the first section of the beach I spotted a young
seagull at water's edge. It sat on the wet sand, oddly quiet. Several months
prior, Natalie and I had found a surf scoter, as though she had just been
swept ashore. She didn't walk or fly off when my wife approached, and
she only hissed meekly at me before she allowed herself to be carried to
higher grounds, onto a patch of sand surrounded by ice plants. I had
never seen a duck on this beach before, and I didn't know how to proceed.
I continued collecting trash, but my heart wasn't in it. By the end, I knew
that our marriage would suffer if we didn't try to save the bird. It was
plain to see on my wife's face. She wouldn't have put it this way; she was
afraid of words and afraid of her courage and her anger. Because I am a
coward, I have learned to read faces for clues. This time, the message was

written so large, I said, "Let's get a box from the car. I hope we have a box; and let's get the duck."

She wouldn't have divorced me; worse things had happened. But it would have hurt more than a paper cut. Did I want to save the bird? No, I don't think so. I was sure the surf scoter had come to the beach to die, or anyway, had accepted death. But at the bird rescue, a Quonset hut in an ill-maintained compound outside of Santa Rosa, the supervisor put the black duck in an incubator, because she was cold. I hadn't known birds could get cold. I had imbued them with the wisdom to know when it was time to die, but never considered they might end up in bad situations because of stupidity or bad luck.

This time, Natalie wasn't with me, and I didn't have a box in my car. The bird didn't seem hurt, just tired, possibly cold like the scoter, but it scrambled away when I tried to scoop it up. Because I followed the bird, it was hit by a wave and was helplessly dumped ashore a few feet away. After two more minutes, I was finally able to grab it and carry it to the far end of the beach. I released it amid the ubiquitous ice plants, and it hurried off but couldn't take flight. There was no way I could have contained it in the car, and so I continued my walk.

New rocks had broken off the cliff at the north end of the first section of the beach and I barely made it to the next length. Because the tide was coming in, I didn't attempt to walk toward the final leg. In any case, my bag was full, my back and chest wet with sweat despite the low temperatures. I realized I was hungry.

I stopped at a small restaurant on the bay, a place Natalie and I had visited often. I sat on the patio and drank the tolerable coffee. "You're in." Why was I searching for Natalie when she so clearly wanted to get away from me? What right did I have?

I pulled out my phone and typed in the email address of whoever had taken a selfie with my wife. "I'm Natalie's husband," I wrote. "Would you know where my wife is? I just want to know she's safe."

This was a lie. I wanted to know more than that. I wanted to understand. But all that would have to wait. For now, I had to deny that I was interested in finding her. For now, I had to hide my intentions.

*

If you have a memory like mine, you don't forget the unpleasant things you experience in love and friendship. In time, these will come to define the relationships you had with people. Every good memory you are able to pull from one or the other corner of your mind is followed by the scene that concluded this particular love or made you lose your friend. In due time, your mind is overrun by unpleasantness, by constant failure to hold on to people you thought would be there for you forever. Natalie's note that I had found perched on the dining table now cast a shadow. What had she missed during the years we spent together? At what point had it dawned on her that I wasn't enough? That I wasn't the right one? That she had stopped feeling close to me? When had she awakened to find that the man she'd married twenty years prior was someone she couldn't recognize?

Ben Miller's return message arrived sometime that afternoon while I was asleep on the sofa, Tonda, watching over me from his bed. I got up around four o'clock to feed him and Anemone, and after finding my glasses in my office, I retrieved my phone.

"Who is this?" the message read. "I'm sorry but I don't know any Natalie. How did you get my address?"

I typed out another message and attached the selfie, which I had forwarded to my phone. If my wife should access her account, she would notice the betrayal, but I was willing to risk it. She had received several emails since her departure but hadn't answered or written any messages in that time. I tried to convince myself I had the right to investigate what she had left unsecured. I was doing a terrible job, but still, I couldn't continue my life without knowing what had driven her away.

Within ten minutes, Ben had answered. "This photo is a picture of your wife? I googled your name, and it seems you're a real person. Not sure what's going on, but the woman's name is Helen. Come to think of it, I can't be sure it really is. Care to tell me what this is all about? And if that's what you're worried about — we were not romantically involved. No need to show up at my house with a gun."

I asked where he lived and if he might be interested to meet me somewhere and talk over a cup of coffee. This time his response took several hours to arrive. He lived in Petaluma, and if I was available, I could meet him downtown during his lunch break. "I guess I can do this for you," he wrote. "But after we meet, I don't want to hear from you anymore. It's a bit creepy."

*

The whole affair appeared creepy, though I still can't say why. The main reason might have been the shame that reddened my face when I thought of how pathetic my endeavor was. A middle-aged guy looking for a wife who had fallen out of love with him. What could he hope for, this slightly overweight, reasonably fit guy pushing fifty? What insight would he gain from a meeting with a person he hadn't even known existed?

The man who came to my table after getting coffee at the bar was short, and the stubble was gone. My mind had endowed him with all kinds of impressive qualities since the day before, now I was baffled by how little there was to him. Ben Miller was trim but not impressively so. His jawline had seen better days. "You look relatively sane," he said.

"You got coffee first without identifying yourself."

"I wanted to get a good look at the guy who contacts me out of the blue." He spoke with confidence, as though he'd been meeting strangers in coffee shops his whole life. "Your socks match, and I don't think you're carrying a weapon." He wore hiking boots and loose-fitting jeans. An Eddie Bauer vest completed the Northern California look.

"I don't even own one," I said.

"Don't try to be too harmless. Have you ever noticed how creepy people are who are constantly telling others how normal their behavior is? I work in real estate, and when people insist that they are being reasonable or harmless, I let my colleagues handle them. The ones I don't like very much and won't miss in case something happens to them." He opened his wallet and extracted a business card. Ben Miller — his agency operated nationwide.

"I could probably punch you," I said. "If that makes you feel better."

"Much better," Ben replied. "Now I feel almost comfortable."

I took a black-and-white printout of the photo I'd found on Natalie's computer and pushed it across the table. "You guys look happy."

He only glanced at it. "Not what you think."

"What do I think?"

He didn't hesitate, as though he had rehearsed his answer before meeting me. Or maybe this kind of affair was commonplace for him. "You think that there's some connection, a bond of friendship or love between me and your wife." He paused for effect. "There was none. We met, I did her a favor, and I took a picture I wish I hadn't taken."

"Why would she have given you a fake name?"

He looked at the picture of him and Natalie a second time. "Maybe that's who she wanted to be. Natalie is a bit cute, don't you think? It's a girl's name. Helen is a name for someone with resolve and a bit of ice in her bloodstream. Maybe she liked Helen better."

I took the second printout from my bag, the one that showed the brochure advertising Ursa Carmel's services. "You know anything about her?"

This time he seemed much more interested. He pulled the image closer and inspected it thoroughly. "Ursa Carmel," he read. "What do you make of it?"

"I thought you could help me. The message you sent my wife said 'You're in.' I guess I was hoping the photo of you and this image were somehow connected."

He looked at the printout again, and I could tell, or thought I could tell, that he wasn't happy about looking at the brochure. But he didn't voice any suspicion or disappointment, merely shrugged. "Mysterious," he said.

"What did you mean by 'You're in'? What kind of favor did she ask of you?"

He looked at me as though he had just now realized he wasn't sitting by himself at this particular table in this particular coffee shop. "I know how lame this must sound to a guy whose wife has run off, but I'm not sure anymore. Look, I'm a real estate agent, and I do think..." He trailed off, looked out the large window facing the busy street. "She was looking for an apartment, and, you know, I don't do apartments, and I don't even know anymore how we met up, but she wanted a view of the ocean, she said, and I knew someone who had bought some condominiums in West County and was looking to lease a few of them, and I got her in contact with that guy." He paused, apparently exhausted by his recollections. "What do you want me to say? I helped her get in contact with a guy who was renting out apartments. 'You're in.' I don't know if she ever signed a lease. I don't do leases, but she seemed...in a hurry. She needed a place to stay."

"Why did she contact you? Why you?"

He shrugged his shoulders in that exaggerated way people use to signal they're running out of patience. "A friend might have given her my number. And hey, I'm all over the internet."

"Can you send me the guy's address and number?" I asked. "The guy with the apartment?"

He fixed me in his gaze. "That's not how this works. I'm sorry." With that he got up, and I didn't find the courage to follow him, berate him, beg him, or punch him. I just stared after him, watched him get into a late model Toyota and drive off.

*

My wife had looked for an apartment near the ocean. When had she met Ben? How much time had passed before he sent her the picture with the message that she was "in"? The timeline was imprecise, blurry, but one thing became clear — Natalie had been planning her escape for much longer than I had initially thought. She had looked for ways to leave while still living with me, while having dinner together, while making love to me. Though that expression, making love, was probably not the right one. That recognition hurt too.

Back home, because I dreaded being alone with what was brewing in my head, I fed the dogs, then grabbed my laptop and headed to a hotel bar downtown. I'm not sure what that attraction is, but I've always felt happiest in hotel bars. Maybe it's because there are no regulars — everyone enters the bar at the same level of anonymity. You are a stranger, and within a few days any and all patrons will be swapped out for new ones. No attachments. You can pretend to be someone else without repercussions. Should you strike up a conversation, no one counts on you to tell the truth and nothing but the truth. You are not expected to forge friendships.

I ordered an Old Fashioned and sat at a high table near the glass doors leading out to the patio. The pool was now closed and the lounge chairs were empty. A few guests sat at the bar watching a Giants game.

Ben Miller had googled my name. There was nothing suspicious about that — I had attempted the same, though there had been too many Ben Millers for me to find anything useful. Yet now I knew his agency and location, and I typed what I knew into the search bar.

To say you're a real-estate agent is a little like professing you're a subcontractor or a handyman. It leaves a lot to one's imagination. And after spending two more Old Fashioneds in front of the computer, I was certain that Ben Miller, the real estate agent, did not exist. The agency didn't list any Ben Millers in their directory. I searched all over Sonoma County and then ventured into Marin. After one more drink, I tore up the card Ben Miller had given me that afternoon. I was convinced that if the card was a fake, the name had to be fake as well. And I had no reason to think that anything the man had told me was true.

Instead of driving home, I paid for a room, a toothbrush, toothpaste, and mouthwash, and went up to the third floor. The sheets were crisp, and from the window I had a view of a small pavilion and the Santa Rosa creek. From the window it looked nearly beautiful.

*

Loving and living with someone provides you with moments that seem to stand for something much larger. When I had met Natalie — she was twenty-three and I nearly thirty — she'd felt self-conscious about some warts on her fingers. Not many, but enough that at some point early in our marriage she started to seek help from dermatologists. They prescribed ointments, they froze the warts, but nothing helped for very long. Then, shortly after moving from Chicago to Los Angeles, she developed a wart at the rim of her right nostril. It looked as though a bugger was barely showing.

One late afternoon, I told her to hold still, got my nail clippers from the bathroom and clipped off the wart. It was an amazingly clean cut, taking off the whole wart without cutting into the nose. Afterwards, we were both surprised she'd let me do this. She was squeamish, she hated pain. Any kind of pain, even in short, manageable bursts.

The wart didn't grow back. Not only that, but the warts on her fingers disappeared as well. Twenty years later, they still hadn't returned. Each time we remembered the episode we laughed. The story didn't have any meaning, and on closer inspection only appeared trivial. Still, with other, similar episodes, it had formed our secret language. Now that language had died.

*

Tonda had defecated in the living room and looked at once defiant and apologetic. I let him and Anemone into the yard before cleaning up. The sun was still refusing to show; the neighbors' chickens were clucking frantically. I filled the dogs' dishes and watched them eat, too tired and worn not to enjoy their company.

In the afternoon, I drove to Rohnert Park, the town of alphabet sections and cul-de-sacs. A planned city full of generic developments, it hadn't gained any charm in the sixty years of its existence. If not for the weather, the lack of mosquitoes, and the occasional palm tree, you'd never have assumed you were in Northern California.

Sonia and Craig lived in a small, one-story house in H-section. From their back patio you could see the mountains during the winter months, when their neighbors' trees had lost their leaves. I hadn't known if either of them would be home, yet when I pulled up along the curb, Sonia was pulling weeds in the front yard. She wore a wide-brimmed head and long sleeves, and only turned her head after I locked the car.

Sonia stood slowly, stiffly, and looked at me as though I might try to sell her solar panels or a cheap electricity plan. She was Natalie's age and height, and when they had gone to parties together, you might have thought them sisters. "You shouldn't have," she said. "I have nothing to tell you."

"If you're still in contact with Natalie, could you please ask her to let me know that she's doing fine?"

"I'm not in contact with her. Why shouldn't she be okay? What have you done to her?"

As though he had been waiting for his cue, Craig appeared a moment later. He had gained weight in the last few years, and he walked as if each step made him uncomfortable. "What's this about? Are you trying to cause trouble?" His voice was loud, his tone sharp, as though he wanted to alarm his neighbors. "We've already talked on the phone. There's nothing more to say."

I must have stood silent and rooted to the ground for nearly two minutes, the change in their behavior toward me was too much. Craig and Sonia had often come to our house, we had drunk bourbon until the wee hours of the night. "I don't understand," I finally squeezed out.

"Isn't it clear?" he said. "It's clear to us. Natalie was afraid of you. She doesn't want you to know where she is. And frankly, I would prefer if you left right this minute. I might have to call the cops if you don't."

I was about to turn and get in the car, too stunned to get out another word, another question, but I caught Sonia's expression from the corner of my eye. She seemed pained by Craig's words, and she had slung her arms around herself.

"I'm leaving," I said quickly, "but just one last question. Who is this healer? Who is Ursa Carmel?" I was speaking to Sonia, hoping for some explanation. But she only shook her head. "I don't know her. I've never seen her."

This is where this story should have ended. I drove home, and over the next few days I started to paint again, filling canvases in the ways I knew would sell. I had local and regional admirers, and after several years of wildfires and of the global pandemic, tourists started to return to our county. Business was good enough.

The story would have ended with that confrontation in Craig and Sonia's front yard. I had exhausted my options, and short of hiring a private investigator, there was nothing I could do to reconnect with Natalie. Only she could decide when to reappear in my life, if she wanted to reappear at all. That's what I thought. That's what I told myself when I drank too much. I told myself that a lot.

2

Nine or ten days after driving down to Rohnert Park, the doorbell rang. Or maybe the police just knocked on the door. I was in my garage, finishing a canvas I called "7:10 Tuesday morning," when the dogs' prolonged barking made me drop brush and scraper and walk into the living room. I pulled back the entrance door curtain, and there they stood. Immediately I thought of Craig and his veiled threats. Had he informed the police of Natalie's disappearance? Had he implicated me?

My hand left a red smear on the door handle, and awkwardly I wiped it on my overalls. Then I grabbed Tonda before he could hurl himself at the first officer. "Can I help you?" I said, reciting words I had heard on TV a thousand times, never in real life.

"Are you Mr. Gray Harden?" the officer asked. He wasn't old, though no longer fresh-faced. He was maybe six feet tall and wore black slacks and a leather jacket. What gave him away was the uniformed officer behind him. If not for his presence and the unmarked Dodge behind them, the man who stretched out a hand toward Tonda to let himself be sniffed could have been a guy managing an import/export business. "I'm Detective Glasgow, and this is Officer Raley."

I answered in the affirmative, then looked at my overalls covered in mostly red paint. "I was working," I said.

"We would like you to come with us. We have reason to believe..."

He said more than that, I am certain, and yet I cannot remember a single cliché, not a single phrase. Whatever he might have said is lost now. And still, I knew immediately what he meant, though I had never, not once, thought it would come to this. Natalie had left me to live her own life, no to die. The officers waited in the living room while I changed my clothes. Anemone kept growling at them and wouldn't be appeased, but Tonda didn't make a sound, having decided that the visitors meant no harm to me.

I'm not sure why I didn't ask more questions in the car. And in hindsight, I understand how pitiful my attempts at finding my wife must have appeared. Had I tried hard enough? And why not? Sitting in the back of the Dodge, why didn't I want to know more about what I was about to witness. I felt cold and I was sweating, and I looked out of the window at my neighborhood and couldn't recognize a thing. This wasn't the life I had wanted; this wasn't the city where I belonged. I wasn't even sure why I was stuck in this particular body and who was making these pointless observations.

"When did you last see your wife?" the plainclothes officer asked in a low voice.

"Three weeks ago," I said. "Yes, three and a half weeks ago."

"You didn't file a missing person's report."

"She's not missing," I said, sharper than intended. "She left me. She up and left. One day she was there and the next day she wasn't. She left me a note. She didn't even talk to me."

"That must have made you angry." The guy turned to face me, his clean-shaven face expressing something that might have been pity. It might have been contempt. It could have been suspicion.

"It killed me," I said. "It made me sad."

He grunted and turned around again. The drive to the coroner's office was short; Natalie and I had passed it countless times on guilty pleasure trips to our favorite burger joint. As soon as we entered the building, the uniformed officer disappeared, and the man who had identified himself as Detective Glasgow led me down a dark hallway before opening a door to his right.

A woman dressed in a white coat, white cap, and white mask, greeted us and walked ahead of us to a row of stainless-steel doors. I had only been once or twice inside a police station — once to get permission to hold a race in my neighborhood when I was a teenager — and never in a coroner's office; I had seen these places merely on-screen. It made the experience unreal, as though I were just playing a husband asked to identify his wife. Only the smell, this odd mixture of lab and hospital smells, of disinfectants and decay, drove home the point that I wasn't playing make-believe. Still, my mind couldn't accept any of what I saw in the next few moments, and I couldn't feel a thing, though I was able to nod, I was able to tell the woman in white and the detective that yes, this was my wife, though the face didn't resemble Natalie's any longer. There were no outside wounds, no damage had been inflicted, yet everything that had made her the person I loved had left the body. If not for the small scar above her right eye — a car accident some years before we had met — and her triple-pierced earlobes, I would have sworn this body had never belonged to the person I had been married to for twenty years.

"The next step will be hard," the detective said, then fell silent, obviously searching for the right words. "There are a few abnormalities. We noticed that someone shaved the entire body, after her death. They cut her nails too. She was bathed and her skin painted."

"Painted?"

"What you'll see is gruesome. The body has been made to look as though its decay is in an advanced state. I know what it must sound like to you, but even though it doesn't make sense, there was something...loving...about the arrangement. As though somebody who cared had sent her off and made sure she would be safe."

It wasn't laughter that came from my throat, it couldn't have been. But the detective's gaze sharpened, and he quickly pulled back the sheet covering Natalie's body.

He had been right. The sight was gruesome. Natalie's skin looked bluish and green in places; in others it had been painted a dark purple. Scarlet areas resembling violent wounds covered some of her torso, as though to indicate the places where predators had torn into the corpse.

I waited for myself to cry, scream, to sob, but none of that happened. Yes, I was there, I registered what coroner and detective asked and said, yet I was not participating, only watching. The ghastly paint on Natalie's body took away anything I could describe as feeling. I wasn't looking at my wife but at a depiction of death. Someone else took over for me, someone else answered questions. Later, much later, I remembered hearing the woman talking about burst vessels or organs, but by then I wasn't sure what the context had been. I couldn't remember her voice or eyes, I couldn't remember how I had left the station, and how I had ended up in an office overlooking the parking lot, sounds of the traffic on the 101 stealing past the old window.

"You know I have to ask some questions. You're not a suspect, you're free to stay silent and leave at any point in our conversation."

"Where did you find her?"

He didn't answer right away. Instead, he pulled a pack of Parliaments from his desk and offered. I hadn't smoked in years, but I took the lighter from his hand and got the cigarette going after the fourth try. He lit up as well, and together we smoked for a few moments before he asked, "Where do you think we should have found her?"

I understood the implications but couldn't muster any outrage. I couldn't feel my fingers, I couldn't feel my feet. "I don't know. Maybe near the water. A guy I met, a guy with a fake name, he said Natalie had been looking for an apartment."

"A guy with a fake name?"

I don't think the room was wired for interrogations, nor did it feel like the detective's personal office, despite the cigarettes. "What is this?" I asked stupidly, waving my hand around, dropping ash to the ground.

"Someone left, never returned. We're understaffed. We have more offices than officers. What was the guy's fake name?"

"Ben Miller." I told Glasgow about the photo he'd taken, the cryptic message, and how we had met in a coffee shop.

"Sounds fishy," the detective said after I had finished my account.

"What he told me or what I'm telling you?"

He didn't answer, just took a last drag and lit a second cigarette. "A hotel room in town." He named the place, a new, somewhat upscale place downtown, one side looking out onto the 101. "We have requested security footage, but there seems to be a problem. She didn't sign in herself. In fact, nobody signed in for the room she was found in. A new arrival got the scare of his life."

"How did she die?"

"You didn't listen. I didn't think you heard a single word. The coroner isn't sure yet. There are burst vessels in her head, in her body. Organ rupture. But she doesn't know what might have caused those. We haven't found anything on her, no contusions, no signs of violence. Her purse was on the nightstand. The only thing in her wallet was her ID. Everything else is gone."

"How long has she been dead?"

"Four to five days. Maybe a bit longer. We think someone kept the body refrigerated before leaving it in the hotel room." He offered me a second cigarette, but I declined. I felt sick, and a headache was announcing itself. "Why did she leave you?"

"I'm not the man she married. She wasn't the woman I had married anymore either. We missed the point where we headed in different directions."

"We'd like to take a look at your wife's belongings."

"Yes, of course. Right now?"

"If you don't mind."

*

I sat with the dogs in the backyard while the officers searched Natalie's room, our bedroom, the garage, the kitchen. By then it was near evening, the sun no longer singeing lawn and bushes. I had poured myself a drink and didn't touch it. From time to time the dogs whined and barked at the sounds coming from inside the house, and the neighbor next door, the one with the chickens, yelled at his children.

It was almost six o'clock when Glasgow stepped out onto the patio and announced that they were leaving.

"Found anything?" I asked.

"You were close."

"Yes," I said. "Yes, we were."

"We'll run the photo of the man who identified himself as Ben Miller through our database, though I'm certain there's not enough to get any kind of match."

"Don't forget Ursa Carmel," I said.

"Another fake name."

"Yes, another fake name. I'm sure that my wife contacted her."

"Why?"

I shrugged. "I know it sounds implausible. New-agey. But my wife was searching for who she might become. She didn't trust herself to find what she was looking for. A healer or wise woman, whatever you want to call her, would have been tempting."

"Do you have any idea where this person might have held her retreat?"

I shook my head. "I wouldn't be surprised if it had been scheduled in the Catskills or near Yosemite. Or in Oaxaca for that matter. These types of retreats often choose destination locations."

"And you know that because…"

"That's where I used to make my best sales."

He stood there, nodding, seemingly lost in thought. Sunlight was creeping toward the fences; a breeze had arrived and was now rattling the umbrella. "How far did your wife's interest in what you call new-agey go?"

I shrugged. "She's not naïve. She wouldn't fall for obvious scams." But I remembered a scene from a few months earlier, when she had asked me what I thought about the afterlife and was I prepared for it? I hadn't thought of that evening since, couldn't recall what had led to her question. I told Glasgow about it, feeling embarrassed.

"And what did you answer?" he said without changing his expression, which was really no expression at all.

"I said that I didn't believe in an afterlife. None at all. You're alive, and one day everything that was you is gone."

Rather than walking away, he sat down on the steps, squinting into the evening sky. "You might read in the paper about this if the captain decides to talk. So I will tell you first, as a kind of courtesy. There's one more thing."

"One more."

"The painting of the body suggested decay. It's...you can research it, but it's reminiscent of a Japanese tradition called Kusôzu. It was a popular genre until the 19th century, and it depicted mostly women."

"And that's what you couldn't say at the coroner's office?"

He shook his head. "Kusôzu is a tradition of painting, it's usually not done on the body itself." Tonda approached the detective, and Glasgow started pulling at his ears. "But we don't know how it fits in with your wife's death. There was another anomaly, though. Her feet. You didn't ask to see them, and I had advised the coroner not to reveal them."

I sat very still, I remember, and my body felt as though it was hovering above ground without the help of the chair, the way your body might feel when you fall asleep at night, your right hand in your wife's left. "Why is that?"

"They are missing. They were cut off after her death." Glasgow didn't look my way, merely continued scratching Tonda's head. After a minute he decided not to wait for my question; he must have known none was coming. He left me his card and apologized for the mess his officers had no time to clean up. He acted sympathetic in that trained way now, firm and breezy, the same way every counselor and therapist appears sympathetic. He petted Tonda one last time and turned to leave. "I'll be in touch," he said. "Don't go anywhere."

*

After two more days I took a hammer to my phone. The captain had indeed decided to talk, announcing that I wasn't a suspect yet. That 'yet' gave the press just enough to follow my every step and wait in front of the house all day. A less dramatic gesture might have sufficed, but after the first twelve hours of being besieged by people who wanted to look into my past and find the reason why I had murdered Natalie, I needed that gesture. I still hadn't talked to Natalie's parents, and I already knew that I never would. They had moved to Phoenix in old age and were consumed by pickle ball and short hikes in the desert. Vodka and Scotch filled their afternoons. Natalie had visited them once or twice a year, to make sure she didn't miss their last years on the planet. I, however, for one reason and two and three others, hadn't seen them in years. My own parents had died long after I had stopped calling them. I wasn't given the family gene; I still had nightmares about being a child in Northern Michigan.

Not even the backyard proved safe as long as my neighbor was at work; everybody wanted a glimpse, a statement. Someone at the station had leaked a photo of Natalie's body, though mercifully one that omitted the ankles; reporters must have hoped for me to confess. I was a painter, surely I had something to do with the paint that turned her body into a fearsome object. Natalie had left me, and this was how I had taken my revenge.

The fear of being mistaken for a murderer proved debilitating at times. It was hard to get dressed, harder even to get undressed. I didn't take the dogs for their twice-daily walks, my world shrank. What stands out for me from that time is the knowledge that I was losing my memories of Natalie. To be more precise, the sight of my dead wife had already begun to alter the memories I had of my years with her. I had dreams of Natalie sitting on our sofa cross-legged, her feet missing. When I thought of a past trip to New Mexico for a friend's wedding, Natalie — who had never considered getting a tattoo — now was covered in small images of wolves with their fangs bared, of eagles with their talons ready to strike. Every single memory I had of making love to my wife now ended with her cold, discolored skin waking me from my reveries.

I didn't stop after destroying my phone. I ripped off the doorbell, hid in my bedroom. On the local news I could see my neighbors talking to journalists. "They seemed happy," they said. "He was very distant, very private. We never understood what kind of business he was running." We'd never had a landline, so after phone and doorbell there was nothing else to smash. I didn't have any answers for anybody, and to distance myself from the headlines in the local paper and TV coverage, I packed a bag. Two more days went by before I could even poke my head out of my front door. Then the vans and cameras disappeared. I had no idea where else I wanted to be, but I needed to leave before the police could dig up new evidence and send reporters back into my neighborhood.

Sonia sat in her car blocking the driveway when I opened the garage door. I didn't know how long she'd been there, and at first she didn't react, as though she might not have heard or seen me. I pulled open the passenger door. Her face was very white, and for once she wasn't wearing any make-up. Only after the third time did she answer my question by getting out of the driver's seat and following me inside.

"I'm afraid," she said after I had put some bourbon in front of her. She sat with her heels on the loveseat, as though she might be perched on a branch or rock. "I knew something bad would happen."

I took one of the armchairs, could barely contain my anger. "But you didn't tell anyone."

"I couldn't be sure. I wasn't sure. It's not like I had any evidence."

"But you didn't tell anyone."

She looked at me like a blind person, like she couldn't make out who was talking. She turned toward the sound. "She had already left you."

"Craig?"

"He had no idea. If I had told him about my fears, he would have thought Natalie insane. He would have thought me insane."

"Why would he think that?"

She pulled a brochure from her bag and slid it across the table. It was the same Natalie had taken a picture of. I turned it, opened it, but apart from some pictures of a sentimental nature — foggy mountains, deep-green forests — there was very little to explain what exactly Ursa Carmel was offering. There was no phone number, no email, no mailing address.

"How did you get this?"

"It sounds stupid," Sonia said. "You won't believe me. And you might be...you won't..." I didn't respond, didn't urge her to reveal how she had come into possession of the brochure, and after a minute or two, she had her voice under control again. "It's been almost a year. Nat and I went to the Flamingo in July or August, and I think she realized that she needed a change in her life. She said something to that effect, like 'I need to find out what it is I'm meant to do or meant to be.' Something like that." They had been sitting by the pool when two men approached them and asked their names. "For a moment I thought they were looking for Nat, as though the three had agreed to meet. But the two men said they'd never been to California before and then asked us if they could buy us drinks, and I forgot about that thought. We had fun. They were staying at the hotel, some business meeting in town, and after a while we went to their suite and had several more drinks. We had fun, we..." Sonia looked up from her fingers which lay stretched out on the table. "I think she enjoyed it more than she had thought. I lost track of her for an hour or two, but we talked the next day, and she didn't feel guilty at all." She paused again. "I'm sorry. But I think she realized she had been missing something. I mean she wasn't in love with the guy, but something, I don't know, something changed. She was changed after that."

"And that man gave her the brochure?"

She shook her head. "Not right away. But a week or so later he called Nat, and she agreed to meet him." She stopped, putting a hand over her mouth, then slowly removing it again. "I'm so sorry, this must be so awful for you to hear." But without waiting for me to respond, she continued. "I remember Nat was very upset later. She called me the next day. Something went wrong; the guy didn't appear to be..."

"Does that guy have a name?"

Sonia grinned sheepishly. "I don't remember his name, it wasn't memorable."

"Something changed, she was changed — and you don't even remember his name?"

"It wasn't like that. It wasn't the guy she was after, she wasn't. But...he'd made something happen. She suddenly thought about her own life, about what kind of life was ahead of her, and I think she was scared." She fell silent, and I used that moment to get up and refresh our drinks, but she didn't even look at her glass. "Anyway, they were supposed to meet at a restaurant, and the guy shows but halfway through the dinner, he starts to ask her all kinds of questions."

"All kinds of questions," I echoed.

"About what kind of life she's leading, and about the fire, and about being true to herself. He says meeting her wasn't a coincidence."

"The fire?"

"She might have mentioned that at the Flamingo, I don't know. Nat is taken aback. She thinks this is an illicit rendezvous, and instead the guy suddenly turns all serious as though he's some kind of therapist or guru. She gets so irritated, she grabs her things and is ready to leave, but the guy says, no, it's important that she hear him out, and when Nat doesn't want to listen, he gives her the brochure."

"Who is this Ursa Carmel?"

"We never found out. Nat left on the spot, and we looked at the brochure the next evening — she picked me up after work — and we had to laugh at how amateurish the material was. The tacky pictures, the lack of a contact address." Only now did Sonia become aware of the glass in front of her, and she drank quickly. After that evening, she had kept the brochure, and neither woman expected to hear about it again. But three months before she'd left me, Natalie had asked about the brochure again, and after looking through old magazines and bills and newspapers, Sonia had finally located it. "Natalie seemed relieved. Really relieved, but she didn't want to keep it, she just took a picture."

"Did she tell you why?"

Sonia kept quiet, biting her lips, as though the effort of remembering was causing her pain. "No, but I had the feeling that she had maybe been contacted? Or that she had found out about that healer and was interested in meeting her? Somehow, she didn't seem upset about the episode at the restaurant anymore. But she didn't answer any of my questions. She took the photo and then she switched the topic."

I went to my office and came back with a photo of the man who had identified himself as Ben Miller. "Do you know him?" I asked.

She studied the image, then shrugged. "It could be him; I don't know. He wasn't wearing sunglasses and hat when I saw him."

"Did you know that Natalie was thinking about renting a place in Sebastopol?"

"No, she never said anything to me. She didn't say a thing about when she was going to leave you."

We sat at the kitchen table until the sky no longer held any light and the city around us ignited its blaze. In the distance, someone's souped-up engine roared briefly.

"Why did you come?" I asked. "Why are you telling me this? You don't know the names of the men, and you don't know anything about the healer."

She nodded. "I just didn't want you to think I don't care about what happened to Nat. I do, and I did want to help you, but..." She didn't finish the sentence. Tears began to wet her cheeks, and she strangled small noises before they could gain the upper hand. I went into the kitchen and returned with a handful of paper towels. Sonia thanked me, wiped her eyes, nose, and finally looked at her watch, a small golden thing she wore on the inside of her wrist. "Craig can't know I saw you. If he calls, please don't tell him. And please, don't tell the police. I don't want to talk to them, I don't want to tell them about Nat and her affair. It seems so cruel and unnecessary." She grabbed her purse and slowly got up. "I should have said something earlier, but she was my friend. I couldn't betray her."

"Does Craig know about what happened at the Flamingo?"

She seemed surprised rather than anxious, and in the semi-darkness I meant to see a brief smile pulling at the corners of her mouth. "Oh, he doesn't, but he wouldn't mind."

She opened the door and walked back to her car. I stood watching her throw the purse in the backseat and get behind the wheel. Then music became audible from within the car. In another minute she was gone.

*

I've often been rejected by the women I fell for. Often enough I wasn't. I haven't kept count; pride and eagerness to feel loved won't allow for certain memories to be kept on shelves, though I have started to wonder when exactly I grew convinced that I couldn't be loved. In my teens, in a provincial town in Michigan? Most likely. In my twenties, after moving to Los Angeles, I became accustomed to women and men approaching me with obvious interest. But the thought that someone could stick around and keep loving me for more than a few weeks seemed like too much to ask. Soon enough, I felt, women would see me for who I was and lose interest. And who was I? I had little curiosity and little passion outside of wanting to become a painter. I didn't read enough, I didn't study hard enough. I was driven merely by the wish to belong, to find a place I could call my own and that nobody else wanted badly enough to fight me for it.

Natalie hadn't been impressed by my paintings, not even when I was fresh out of art school and still imagining a future with retrospectives of my work in major museums around the world. She liked them, she was okay with them, but she showed no particular love for the grays and whites and blacks I used, somber canvases that a gallerist had described as too bleak and sinister to be commercially viable. Sometimes emaciated or bloated figures occupied the corners of my paintings, but often the spaces were uninhabited, as though the last people on earth had chosen death rather than keep living an existence devoid of color. I thought those paintings beautiful and producing them filled me with an ecstasy only nights on rooftops in Culver City, in the arms of whoever I had met an hour or two ago, could equal.

After meeting Natalie, the darkness flattened out, and my palette changed. For a while, opulent nudes caught the eye of some critics, but it was the art fair circuit that fell in love with me. They fell in love with what I produced after a friend had invited me to sell paintings from his booth. These were the same visions that had once haunted me, only now I used gaudy colors. A practical joke is what I was shooting for, but during that first weekend at a San Diego Art Fair I made more money from my work than I had earned the previous year waiting tables. I was hooked. People might not have loved my work, but they liked it well enough to pay too much money on a hazy afternoon.

*

The next two weeks I stayed in Reno, on the outskirts of town. Hugo, a painter I knew from my days traveling the country, let me stay while he was visiting art fairs in the Midwest and South. The house stood on seven acres of dirt, with a large, barn-like structure in back.

My friend's house was plain and without much charm, but the studio out back was lavishly appointed and full of life. A bathroom and shower with gold handles, gilt mirrors, and a golden toilet had been added to the utilitarian structure. The main room had two parts — one was his paint-splattered workspace, the other held several black leather couches, a large coffee table with drawers full of drug paraphernalia, and shelves full of books and art objects, mostly antique and expensive. The backwall of that part was taken up by a large bar, ripped, it appeared, from an old saloon. He'd left enough bottles on the shelves to last me many months.

That first day in Reno, I sat with the dogs in the studio, unsure of what to do. I drank, I walked the perimeter of the property, I played fetch with Tonda and Anemone. On the second day, I moved into the studio and began to draw. Rather than smearing thick layers of paint on large canvases, I bought several sketch pads and drew in pencil and charcoal. I drew the dogs who seemed besotted with their new life, eager to make the fenced-in property theirs. Trees shielded us from the neighbors. The road in front of the house stayed empty most of the day.

Soon though, Natalie began to appear on those sheets. Natalie sitting naked in front of a window in Vegas, Natalie asleep in her car seat, Natalie studying a book. I drank my friend's bourbon and drew. I slept when I got too drunk and continued drawing after waking up again. Often, it was the dogs who nudged me awake.

By the end of the first week, the floor of the studio was littered with my versions of Natalie, with the images that floated into my mind whenever I shut my eyes. Maybe it was a purge, but maybe I drew these images because I didn't want to lose her altogether. I wanted to save my version of her, however faulty and inadequate my perception had been.

The booze allowed me to forget about what I had seen at the coroner's office. The booze made me weep while I was creating Natalie's likeness on a flat sheet of paper. As long as I kept drinking and drawing, I didn't think of what had come later. I didn't think of the burned ruins of our house, I didn't force myself to recite her goodbye-note. Her skin remained immaculate, unblemished, unpainted. There's irony in this, that a painter should create memories of his wife before her killers covered her body in paints of decay and decomposition. But booze is no great friend of irony.

To celebrate my week of honest work, work I would never sell, work that existed because I wanted it to exist, not because someone would pay me for it, I ordered three pies of pizza. I shared the food with the dogs and mixed myself several Old Fashioneds.

This time it wasn't the dogs who brought me back to life. "You sounded like you might choke. You stopped breathing after every snore."

I sat up, vaguely alarmed. My friend hadn't said a word about a visitor. But my mind took its time. Instead of answering, I stared at the drawings covering the floor.

"Here." She handed me a glass of bourbon. Another one appeared in her hand momentarily and she sniffed what she had poured. "How do you know Hugo?"

"Who's asking?" The dogs were nowhere to be seen. I looked at my watch, I looked at my rumpled clothes and thought about when I had taken my last shower. I looked at the bourbon in my hand but didn't have the heart. The woman opposite of me took a sip of her drink. She was maybe forty-five, and everything about her seemed very narrow and very long. She looked tall, though it was hard to say now that she was seated. Her nose and lips were thin, her jaw wide. Her nails were short, her fingers full of rings. Little scars crisscrossed the backs of her hands. She wore jeans and a white linen shirt. Or better, a linen shirt that had once been white. Maybe it had been washed with the wrong colors, maybe she had spilled wine on her front and sleeves.

"I'm Beth," she said. "I'm looking for Hugo."

"He's in Ann Arbor, or maybe Columbus."

"And you are?"

I lied. I invented a story I thought was plausible, though at six in the morning I couldn't be sure. The moment I had said my piece I had already forgotten who I was supposed to be. "Have you seen my dogs?"

She looked surprised. "Dogs?"

The alarm I had felt upon waking intensified. This woman, Beth, said something more, but I wasn't listening any longer. I left her draped over the end of a leather couch and through the open door in back I stepped outside. The sun had not yet climbed the mountains; the air was still cool. After living in California for fifteen years, the starkness of the mountains was intimidating. You sensed that people you encountered here would not be pleased with your presence. In these mountains you could hide whatever it was that needed to be hidden.

A few firs lined the left side of Hugo's property, and bushes and small trees covered much of the rest. I called for Tonda and Anemone and received no response. I hadn't heard her steps, had already forgotten about her; Beth's hand touched the small of my back and made me squirm. "You sure about the dogs? That you have any?" I turned to face her, and yes, she was tall, her face level with mine. "You must be Gray, right? I don't think Gray Harden owns any dogs." Her breath smelled sweet, maybe it was the bourbon, or maybe the gum she was chewing now. "Where are her feet?"

"What?" I looked down at the woman's feet. She was wearing flip-flops, her toes as long as my pinkie.

"Not mine. The one you're drawing like a madman. Where are her feet? You must be either newly in love or she gave you the boot. You must have drawn her thirty or forty times, but she doesn't have any feet."

"She doesn't have any feet," I echoed. Then I left her and walked past the barn and past the main house toward the front of the property. My old Mitsubishi still stood where I had parked it, and a Toyota pickup now sat next to it. The gates to the property had been left wide open.

I called for Tonda and Anemone, but there was nothing. I'm not given to superstition or the realm of the supernatural, but even I, still boozy from the night before and out of my wits, could smell how empty the air was. Wherever they had gone, they weren't even close.

Anger heated my body. I stumbled back into the studio, grabbing at the images that covered the floor. As though Beth hadn't already seen them and gone through them all, I gathered and hid them, covering Natalie with a shirt and a drop cloth. "Why did you leave the gate open?" I yelled. My brain was still slow, I still meant to see the woman in the spot where she had put her long hands and long, forceful fingers on me.

I yelled the same question again outside, but only the Toyota's engine answered, and a few seconds later, I could see the truck driving west. In that moment I grew frightened. I couldn't know what any of it meant at the time, or how this episode fit into Natalie's disappearance and death. Still, I was barely able to breathe. I stood in the back of the studio for several minutes, before I walked once again toward the road and left the property to look for my dogs.

*

Hope. I wish people had no hope. Maybe then they would stop washing their cars on Sunday mornings, suds running down the street and into creeks and down to the ocean. Maybe they would save water, maybe they wouldn't dump old tires into rivers. Hope is the credit card of our conscience, much like purgatory. Hope is the purgatory of the living; we sin today and hope that there will be time to turn things around later. Later when we've had enough, achieved enough; later when we've quenched our greed. Hope and greed spring eternal.

I didn't have much hope, but I still had plenty of fear left, which, maybe, is the same thing expressed from two different angles. The same object observed from different corners of a room. I do think that hope is more toxic than the lack thereof. The hopeless — do they go and murder others? The hopeful always do.

"I couldn't have known. How could I have known about the dogs?" She appeared two days later, in the early evening and before you could comfortably walk outside. Her black t-shirt showed how sweaty she was. "Have they returned?"

Anemone had, but Tonda was still missing. By now, I thought, he might have gotten himself killed or newly adopted, it was strictly 50/50.

"You won't let me in?"

I was scared of her and maybe too proud to admit it. "How did you know who I was?"

"I brought pizza and red wine. I want to make amends." She lifted the box, balancing it on her palm. "It's still somewhat hot. I'll tell you if you let me in."

In the end I might have been more afraid of what I didn't know than of this stranger. And maybe I sensed that she hadn't returned merely because I was such great company. She had some message to deliver or some task to accomplish. The smell of the pizza made me nauseous.

"I'm sorry about your dog," she said once she had entered the studio. "I really am. Where are all the pictures?"

She put down the large box on the coffee table and walked to the bar to open the wine. It was a gaudy one-and-a-half liter something or other, the kind of wine you find at gas stations and convenience stores. "Do you smoke?"

"Haven't had a cigarette in years."

"No, I mean, do you want to get stoned?"

"Later maybe."

"Shit, you want to come outside with me at least? I can't have this conversation if I don't get high."

I mixed myself an Old Fashioned and followed her to the back of the property. I had no idea who owned the land beyond the chain-link fence, which rose steadily toward the mountains. No trees obstructed our view, only grasses and bushes dotted the rocks.

Beth sat down, her legs crossed, and lit up. She wore flip-flops again, and her feet looked like impossibly long hands. I put my own hand flat against her right foot. She looked down with interest. "Your conclusion?"

"Why are you here? You don't know Hugo, I'm certain of it."

"You haven't called him?"

"It wouldn't change the situation."

She blew smoke my way, silently laughing. "What is the situation?"

"You want something from me, and I don't know what it is. I can't trust you because you released my dogs. You could have stolen my wallet, my keys, my car, and you didn't. So it's not money you're after. It's not my rugged good looks, it's not my art."

"You don't know about that last one. I might have a job for you."

I sat back and watched her inhale. Anemone came from the barn and lay down in front of us. "What kind of job might that be?" I asked.

"Okay, I don't have a job for you. I can't afford to hire anyone to do anything. I'm here to tell you a story. I should have delivered it last time, that would have been the efficient method, right? But I chickened out, and in any case, you weren't in the mood to listen."

"You should have delivered it last time? It's not your story then. And your name is probably not Beth either."

"It could be Beth. It might be Beth. It fits, doesn't it?"

I nodded.

She put her blunt back into a small metal case, after carefully stubbing it out on the sole of her sandal. "I'm ready," she announced. "Where would you like to listen to my story?" Without waiting for an answer, she got up and strode toward the barn. "Will you mix me a drink? Can I use your bathroom? Wait." She stopped, and the next second, came running back toward me. She grabbed my face and kissed me, then let go just as abruptly. "Yeah, I'd like one of those you're having."

I had the drinks ready when she returned. Outwardly, nothing seemed to have changed about her, but she didn't seem to be the same person she'd been just a few minutes earlier. Maybe it was the weed, or maybe it was my imagination. She seemed more solemn, more deliberate. Maybe she had changed her mind. She took the glass from my hand, kicked off her flip-flops, and sat down on one of the sofas, legs crossed once again. "I know what killed your wife."

I can still feel exactly how my body was situated in the large room, how I held my glass, how I had positioned my feet. I can still feel the warmth of my skin against the old tee I was wearing, a bit of stiffness lingering in my back from sitting on the ground outside and listening to my visitor. Nimble and bendy I had never been.

I can still feel the connection I imagined we had — impossibly trite and incredibly stupid after what had happened — snap abruptly. I can still see the unopened pizza box on the coffee table. I can still hear those first words she spoke.

"How? Why?" I asked.

"I might not be able to answer questions for a while. I'm just here to talk, I was sent to talk, not answer questions."

I sat down across from her. "Who sent you?"

"Who knows? I was given a story and I'm going to tell you now. Listen, Gray, just listen. It's difficult enough the way it is, no need to interrupt and ask me things I know nothing about." That was the beginning. I can't recall what the time was, though it must have been around seven, judging from the light. Maybe eight, no later than that. But by the time she was done, it was past midnight. Twice she went to the bathroom, and each time she came back to sit in the exact same spot she had previously occupied. She sat very upright, though she never looked uncomfortable or intimidated. She didn't seem *worried*. Maybe that's what astonished me the most about the situation. She never seemed worried about what might happen to her, as though she knew she was being watched and that someone or something would come to her rescue should I lose my mind. How could she be so sure?

"Nobody murdered Natalie, you mustn't believe that. I know the police suspects you, and you should be aware of how precarious your situation is. A cuckolded husband, a husband who has been abandoned, he meets his wife and murders her."

"Murders her."

"You shouldn't talk, Gray, you shouldn't. I might lose the thread of my story, and I think you shouldn't want me to lose it." She reached for her glass and took a drink. "There are no suspects other than you. There are images, stories, but nothing that implicates anyone but you. Don't go down that route, because it will only lead to your incarceration. A conviction isn't a sure thing, but it's a distinct possibility. Detective Glasgow is kind, if that's the right word for someone who needs to produce the real culprit. His abilities, however, are limited. His resources are limited. He doesn't like you."

She continued, recalling every detail of how Natalie had been found, how even my friends suspected I had something to do with my wife's murder. I was too stunned, maybe, to interfere. Or maybe I felt guilt gnawing at me. What she described sounded so plausible. It made so much sense. How could I not have been responsible for Natalie's death? All the while, the woman who called herself Beth didn't raise her voice. She didn't make an argument, nor was she trying to persuade me. She merely told me, in a voice that was flat and uninvolved, what she had been instructed to say. "I don't know you," she repeated at times, as if to remind me that she was only a messenger. She was only some stranger with a story.

"You failed as a husband. Not entirely, not disastrously, but after twenty years of living with you, Natalie needed to leave and search for who she was. She had forgotten about herself. There was only you, taking up all that space in her life. Your work, your wellbeing, your whims, and moods. You kept her tied to yourself and manipulated her in ways that benefitted you. She could only see you. You left no room for her."

"But I didn't kill her. I'm not a killer. I didn't cut her feet off."

Beth stopped and looked at me with something like pity or perhaps mild disgust. "It's not about you, it never was. You murdered Natalie some years ago. Just because someone still walks and does their daily chores doesn't mean they are alive. Let's not split hairs over that statement. Can you make me another drink?"

I mixed two Old Fashioneds. I was a bit drunk by then, in a way that loosens your limbs without making you sluggish. I didn't want my drink, but I didn't know how else to keep listening. I wanted to hear what Beth had to say and I needed to fortify myself.

When I returned to the sofa, she was eating pizza from the open box. "It's rather good. You should have a slice." She spoke like the Beth who had arrived earlier that night, before getting stoned and ready to deliver her story. "Your friend has an awfully nice place."

"Where do you live?" I asked.

She cocked her head, a motion that reminded me of Tonda and made me get up to look for Anemone. She sat at the back door, staring out onto the property with half-open eyes. I walked around the house to the front gate, but Tonda hadn't come home. I called his name, convinced for a moment that he had to be close.

"I really am sorry about your dogs."

"You knew about them."

"I did. But how was I supposed to know they'd run off the way they did? You can't blame me for that. Not entirely."

"Who told you? Who told you about me and Natalie and my life?"

She was still chewing pizza, washing the bites down with bourbon. "Nobody. I'm not a person anybody confides in. I'm the kind of person who gets paid to do things. I do them, I'm discreet."

I must have stared at her, because a smile formed on her lips, and she said, "You should see yourself. I'm not a ghost. I have no idea who you are, Gray Harden, but I sure learned a lot about you."

"Someone gave you a script?"

She put a long finger on her thin lips. "Your wife died because she had lost her way. That's why she arrived at their doorstep. She wanted to listen and wanted to hear. That thought filled her and gave her purpose. She was warned, she signed papers that absolve a certain person of all responsibility for the consequences of their encounter."

"Ursa Carmel."

"Ursa Carmel? Sure, why not. Let's call the person Ursa Carmel. Natalie contacted Ursa Carmel because something in her life had gone missing. You might know something about that."

"She wanted to hear? Hear what?"

"You shouldn't interrupt me, you really shouldn't. You had depleted Natalie. Sometimes, when you're very desperate, a teacher will appear. The person you call Ursa made herself known to Natalie, and after some time they met. Natalie prepared herself and signed all the papers. Ursa has a gift and sharing it with the world isn't easy. It has caused her much scorn and harm. She needs to be very careful with whom she interacts. And now she is offering to meet you. It will be on her terms, it will be brief. She doesn't want to be involved in police investigations. She has important things to accomplish, she simply doesn't have time for interrogations, for police snooping around. She's an artist, not a murderer. She fulfilled your wife's one wish. She is not responsible for her death. In exchange for your silence, she will see you."

"And kill me too?"

"Silly. You would be dead already if she wanted you dead. You're not very careful. You can't even take care of your dogs, Gray Harden."

"And how will I meet her, this Ursa Carmel who might not be Ursa Carmel?"

Beth closed her eyes, then slowly rubbed them with the tips of her fingers. "I wasn't told about that part. Only that you will be contacted, the way you were contacted by me."

"And until then I just go about my life? I'll just wait and see who killed my wife?"

"They didn't kill her. You have to let go of that thought. She listened, she heard, and that's all there is to it. Nobody laid hands on Natalie. What she did and the risk she took — she did this of her own free will." She closed her eyes again. "I'm done now. Don't hate me. I just told you what you needed to hear. I'm tired."

Anger suddenly swept over me, closed my throat, and threatened to choke me. With difficulty, I tore myself away from the woman on the couch and walked off into the studio half of the building, trying to breathe and calm myself down. I went to the heap of pictures I had drawn and looked at Natalie and all the moments I remembered from our life together. I had imagined I was caring for her, earning a living so we could live. But a living and life were not necessarily the same. How many years had been good years? When had I started to neglect her? When had I stopped seeing her?

I heard her footsteps, soft, bare, before I felt her arms around me and saw her fingers interlock over my chest. "Don't get any ideas," she said. "This is just an extension of goodwill. A sign that you needn't worry." Her breath on my skin made me shiver. "I'll let you measure my toes. I'll take your measure."

3

August came and went without a message from anyone connected to Ursa Carmel. And since Tonda had appeared the day after Beth left the house for the last time, the whole episode in Reno couldn't find a place to nest in my mind. The memory existed, but no path would lead me to it. After only two or three days of being back in California, Reno had lost all its reality. The pictures I had drawn of Natalie remained, though they seemed to lose their connection to my friend's barn the minute I put them on a shelf inside my studio.

By October, I had given up hope to ever hear from Ursa Carmel. And what danger was I to her? I didn't know her real name, and neither Ben nor Beth had left their address behind. They existed, and yet you couldn't make them appear. They had spun their stories while making sure that I held no valuable information about what had happened to Natalie. They had been clever inventions, actors on a stage with no one taking photographs or keeping record.

Then a bill arrived from a storage facility in Sebastopol. It was addressed to Natalie. I called the manager, explained the situation. He recognized the story from the news, and he agreed to let me have a look as long as I paid the outstanding amount. Two hours later, he unlocked the gate to a mid-size rectangular unit. It turned out that Natalie had first rented the unit over two years prior; if I hadn't contacted him, he would have sold off the contents in another thirty days.

The manager, a middle-aged guy in coveralls, a Giants cap, and steel-toe shoes, seemed afraid I was going to make off with something valuable, so he stayed seated in his golf cart while I was moving through the unit, eyeing me with something between pity, disgust, and greed.

The space was about ten feet wide and fifteen feet long. It contained chairs, a table, a whole dining set, lamps, carpets, and several paintings and prints. At first, I didn't understand. Natalie had left me without taking anything, and to the best of my knowledge, she had never moved into an apartment. Nobody had come forward after her death; certainly, Glasgow would have filled me in. I couldn't even be sure that Natalie had ever tried to set up her own place. The police had never established her whereabouts from the day she left to the day she had been found on the hotel bed.

"You okay?" the manager shouted from outside. Maybe I had been too silent for too long.

"Give me a few more minutes," I shouted back, but my voice quivered. I made my way through the whole unit, lifting this lamp and holding that set of dinner plates. Everything was neatly ordered, nothing had gathered dust, even though I understood that collecting these items had taken her a long time. She had gathered furniture and other furnishings, everything she needed to start a new life. While she was living with me, she had slowly worked toward her disappearance. There would be no drama; once she chose a day, she could leave without ever seeing me again. She wouldn't have to extract anything from the place she had shared with me, she didn't have to take anything, fight over anything. She could just up and leave.

"Let's move," the manager interrupted my thoughts. "You still need to see the other one."

"The other one?"

He locked up after me, then drove us to another row further down the lot. Here the units were much more spacious, the gates tall and wide enough to admit cars and pickup trucks. He sucked in the air after the electrically operated door had come to rest and revealed the inside. "Fuck me," he said. "That's huge."

My first impulse was to run, though I couldn't say whether I wanted to get closer to what stood in front of me or get away. Filling almost the entire space stood a copy of our old house, on a scale of 1:4 or 1:5 maybe. It looked to be made entirely of cardboard and paper, with only an occasional length of wood to provide some needed rigidity. Natalie had painted the outside and inside in the colors we had chosen a year after moving in. But she hadn't stopped there.

A table saw stood in one corner; two large folding tables held an assortment of tools. Walking around the structure, I realized that even our backyard would have proved too small for this replica. Natalie had spent her days in this storage unit, cutting cardboard and wooden planks into the right-size chunks for the walls, cutting out holes for windows. She had used plexiglass for said windows, and left the roof for last, along with the front wall, because after framing and dry-walling and painting the house, she'd made furniture and furnishings from craft paper and poster board. Everything we'd owned, from garage shelves to bookcases, she constructed for the new old house. Natalie had crafted paper rugs and taped them to the bare bamboo floors. The two green and gold comfy chairs, the old blue sofa, the green coffee table we had bought second-hand and which she had loved above all else. You couldn't sit in the cardboard chairs, and the table only supported a few glasses and a plate or two.

She had also recreated the things that had decorated our walls. The painting of a sleeping cat she'd bought at an art opening some years ago. Natalie's drawing wasn't as perfect, as elegant, the colors weren't quite right, but the effect was stunning. An early painting of mine in black and white graced the wall of the recreated living room.

I looked through the open windows and walked several times around the outside of the house to discover all the items she had placed inside. Everything I could remember she had rebuilt. If I'd held a lit match to the structure, everything would have burned within a few seconds.

The manager finally left, maybe sensing that I wasn't going to stiff him on the rent. Or maybe he too felt the strange energy emanating from the house inside the storage unit. The house, recreated to its last detail, had turned into more than a replica. If I had been a religious person, I would have said a prayer.

I pulled a chair, a rickety wooden thing and the only piece of usable furniture, and sat and stared. "Damn you," I muttered. "Damn you."

*

After the fire, only two or three days later, a reporter had called Natalie's number and asked her questions about the night we evacuated. In the article that appeared in the paper some forty-eight hours later, the last quote had read, "I can't be expected to start a new life. Who am I without memories to surround me? I'm not a celebrity, I only ever existed in that house. All I had and was had its place in there. Some days I wake up and can't remember anything."

I must have sat inside the storage unit for over an hour before I noticed an object I didn't remember, one that lay on the coffee table in the living room of the paper house. At first, I had taken it for a recreated book, maybe one of Natalie's beloved cookbooks, but it looked too real. It didn't belong.

It had no dustjacket, and no title was printed or embossed on the black cover. When I opened the book to its first page, it read, *The Nine Thoughts*. I couldn't say why, but I didn't dare leafing through the small book of maybe forty or fifty pages. My hands started to shake.

I closed and locked the unit, paid everything the manager asked for. Sometime later that evening, long after dark, I realized that I was at home sitting in my living room, but I didn't know how I had arrived there. I had no memory of the drive, couldn't have said how long I had been sitting on the sofa with the small volume in my lap. The neighborhood appeared quiet, too quiet, as though everybody had abandoned it. Only a small light in the kitchen — had I forgotten to switch it off this morning? — allowed me to see my surroundings. I failed to recognize them, however, couldn't tell if these were the items that Natalie and I had bought after moving into our rebuilt home, or if some stranger had switched them out for similar items. They had shed their sheen of familiarity and turned to mere objects. I sat among them unnoticed.

*

I should have thought about the next step myself, but it wasn't until Detective Glasgow called in early December that I began to think beyond myself and Natalie. Her paper house kept me under its spell; I visited nearly every week to spend time looking through the windows. At times I meant to remember an appliance or a picture to have taken up a different space, but I couldn't be sure. No photos we had taken of the inside had survived the fire — both of our computers had been destroyed.

The day Glasgow called, he mentioned a possible homicide in London. A British detective had contacted him after remembering having read about Natalie's death. "A coincidence," Glasgow said. "Maybe a lucky break. I'll send you the link and the statements of the family. Look if you can find any similarities, outside the obvious ones. Anything that might ring a bell."

I went into my office and opened the attachments he had sent. The first was a clip from a British newspaper. The body of a teenage boy had been found. He had arrived in London by train, because, as he had told his parents back in Cambridge, he wanted to see the Hawksmoor churches. Being themselves avid fans of Peter Ackroyd's books, the parents had not raised any objections. They paid for the ticket and three nights at a hotel, for their son and a good friend of his. It was their son's 17th birthday, and they trusted his judgment. He was a diligent and a promising student who had been accepted to Queen's College. He had earned a bit of fun.

Farid had gone missing hours after the two boys arrived in the capital. He'd left their hotel room to check out the guest laundry and ask about where he could print pages from his computer — he was working on a paper about incest in Edgar Allan Poe's stories. The other boy, Gavin, having smuggled several small liquor bottles onto the train and consumed them in the bathroom, slept the whole afternoon and woke at eleven that night. His friend had not returned. Gavin didn't call the parents immediately. He was scared he'd be found responsible — after all, he shouldn't have been drinking. He should have been awake to notice his friend's absence. Instead, he left the hotel room and wandered the streets, calling his friend's cell every thirty minutes. Only when he returned to the hotel did he notice that his friend's phone was still in their shared room.

It took Gavin another day to contact his and his friend's parents. The police were called, and officers started to search for Farid. A week later they found him in a hotel in Brighton, two or three minutes from the beach. He looked peaceful, well-groomed and cared for. His hair had been neatly cut. His body had been painted to resemble excessive decay. His feet had been expertly severed and couldn't be found.

The last attachment, a cellphone picture, contained jotted-down notes, presumably in Glasgow's handwriting. According to these, the boy hadn't suffered any outward injuries, no cuts, no contusions, nothing to suggest foul play. Several inner organs had burst.

The last line read, "Check Harden's whereabouts."

In response, I sent him a drawing of Beth. The way I remembered her sitting on the couch talking about why Natalie had been found dead.

There had been no love between me and Beth, and still, at odd moments of the day, I'd sit down and sketch her face. The time spent with her had been transactional — her presence for my silence — but that didn't mean I hadn't felt anything. On some days I felt so ashamed I wanted to burn my sketches, on others I told myself that because I hadn't known her for more than a few hours, I had known her more fully.

A few days later, the detective paid me a visit with several mugshots of women that Reno's police department had sent him. It was late afternoon and had been dark for hours. I had set up an old Christmas tree in the living room, and when Glasgow arrived, I made a fresh pot of coffee.

For several minutes we sat at the kitchen table, and I looked through a binder of photographs. My heart was beating as though Beth had announced her arrival, a stupid and dastardly reaction. Every page I turned was a new promise, a new hope. But her face wasn't among the photos. "She might not have been from Reno," I said.

He nodded. "We haven't had any luck with your fake real estate agent either. Nothing. He might not have been from here."

"How did they die?"

"Doesn't matter," he said. "Who cut off their feet? What for?"

"Any luck with that other boy? Does he remember anything about the day his friend went missing?"

"What teenager would leave his phone behind? He never asked the front desk about printing that paper on Poe. We searched his laptop and couldn't find it. He obviously lied about that too. But why? Where did he really go and who did he meet? It looks as though he lied to his parents about his real motives, but we can't figure out why. He wasn't very active on social media — we've combed through his contacts, but there's nothing to suggest he was being groomed and lured to London."

"No brochure?"

"Teenage boys don't fall for healers, do they?"

"They might fall for something else. A story, some tale that makes their involvement seem important."

He looked at me for a long time, his face not giving away much of anything. "So this person, this Beth, just came to your place, which wasn't even your place, let your dogs get away, and then told you a story about why your wife died and left?"

"Pretty much."

"You're not leaving anything out?"

"Like what?"

"The moment when you ask where the hell your wife's feet are?"

It took courage, courage I couldn't feel but replaced with arrogance, to not look away. "I know she wouldn't answer."

"But you didn't ask."

"I was too stunned. If someone came to you and told you that your wife left because you were a piece of shit and got herself killed because you had robbed her of her spirituality, would you ask about her feet?"

His answer came quickly. "Yes, because that speech wouldn't surprise me one bit. But you thought better of yourself. More highly. You really were surprised."

"Not surprised. I felt caught."

We drank our coffee and didn't say anything more for several minutes. The Christmas tree made the house feel charming, the dogs lying on their beds and eyeing us from time to time made the house feel warm. It was a nice house, a calm house. I was glad I had company, someone who still suspected me and made me feel seen. Beth had caught me unawares with her accusations; the detective enjoyed no such advantage. Almost against my own will, I pulled out my phone and showed him images of Natalie's paper house. He swiped through them in silence, back and forth. At last, he said, "And she did this when?"

"She might have started right after the fire. It must have taken her months, years even."

"It must have cost quite a bit to build this. You never noticed?"

"She was our accountant. She was good with money. I never checked until after she left me."

Glasgow scrolled through the pictures again. "I'll let you know should I find anything," he finally said.

"If you find more severed feet."

Glasgow didn't answer and let himself out. It was the sixteenth of December.

*

I had no intention of scouring the internet for mysterious deaths and severed feet, but that's exactly what I started doing the next day. It was a hum that led me there, a tinnitus-like sound that wouldn't leave my ears.

I had been hearing that sound ever since Beth entered my friend's house with pizza and wine, but until now I hadn't given it any thought. I hadn't really noticed its presence until after Glasgow left and I was sitting by myself at the dining table, my stomach sour from too much coffee, my mind scrubbed clean by the black liquid. Whoever was behind my wife's death, they were still at work, stretching out their feelers and looking for people desperate enough to become interested in their lies. They were at work while I tried to look outside into the backyard and only caught sight of myself, reflected in the glass of the patio doors.

The problem with my internet search wasn't a dearth of entries but a glut of them. Apparently, severed feet had been found on a beach near Vancouver, in parks in Hungary, and on every continent. Theories abounded, some finds were debunked as hoaxes, but there was no lack of severed feet appearing in odd places. Only a few, though, were found close to the body of the victim. In such cases, the perpetrator had cut the corpse into pieces to better get rid of them, or they had been cutting off hands and feet and head to keep the police from identifying the victim.

After a few hours and several cups of coffee I stopped my search and drove to the post office to empty my mailbox. I still enjoyed an almost childlike joy whenever I turned the key and found letters and packages stuffed into the sizeable box. So it was that day. My mood lightened as soon as I pulled out my treasure. I quickly scanned the letters for junk, fit the rest into a bag and went to Whole Foods to purchase ingredients for Christmas dinner. I wouldn't have any guests, but Natalie and I had made it a habit to cook for the dogs and buy them cookies and dog cupcakes. The previous year, she had made a meatloaf for Tonda and Anemone in the shape of a tree. Carrot sticks had substituted for candles.

During my college and grad school days, I had often celebrated Christmas alone without giving it much thought. This year, however, I felt I needed to stock up on everything to keep me from feeling morose. Christmas was a gooey affair, and sooner or later it would find you if you weren't prepared, and it would clog your every pore and choke you.

On the way home, I stopped at the liquor store and made sure I wouldn't run out of bourbon. It was the one way I knew to get out of my head and let things slide when life seemed too dull or too much. I hadn't started to drink until my thirties, when life grew more regulated and Natalie and I stopped moving across the country hunting for a better job, a better city, better friends. The safer our life became, the more anxious

I felt. The house, the cars, the trips, the visits to restaurants and bars — none of it felt substantial. Only bourbon made me accept that nothing I owned or enjoyed would stay with me and that I wouldn't stick around long enough on this planet and in this life to fulfill the odd desires bubbling to the surface every now and then. The desires that had no place in a well-regulated marriage and existence.

The garage door stood open when I returned. Had I forgotten to close it? Had it malfunctioned? The hum in my ears got louder, and I left mail and groceries in the car, checked for missing items in the garage, and then slowly opened the door leading into the house. Tonda came to greet me, and Anemone was snoozing on the sofa barely opening her eyes to glance at me. I sniffed the air, I walked through every room, and even opened the closets. The backyard proved empty as well.

Finally, I unpacked the car, stored meats and produce in the refrigerator, and fed the dogs. It was nearly three o'clock, and since I wouldn't work anymore, I poured myself a drink and sat down on the sofa to open the mail. I leafed through magazines, got sidetracked reading the movie reviews, then returned to bills, registration fees, and requests for paintings. One potential customer had included a photo of the room and wall where he intended to hang my picture, plus the desired measurements. He didn't go as far as requesting certain colors but asked for a muted palette.

I had saved the letters with handwritten envelopes for last. There was something beautiful about them, something charmingly anachronistic. I didn't receive handwritten letters from friends anymore — friends used email or DM'd me when they wanted to get in touch. Only the oldest and youngest customers wrote letters, and their crooked, sometimes lightly smeared lines made me happy. Often their penmanship was nearly illegible, and those letters I cherished the most.

The second or third letter I tore open contained a single, ivory-colored page. It read,

Dear Friend,

My apologies for the delay. Soon I will contact you with a date, time, and address. I will offer you only this one chance at getting the answers you are seeking. If you fail to show, I will assume that you no longer wish to see me.

There was no signature, no name, no "sincerely" or "warmly." When I looked back at the envelope, my name and address were there. The sender's name was E. P. Holst, and the address a street in St. Louis, Missouri. I took out my phone, but even before I typed in the address, I knew this would lead to nothing. The name was an invention, like Ursa Carmel, like Ben Miller, like Beth; she'd never bothered with a last name.

The letter had not been mailed. No stamp graced the envelope, nothing suggested that it had ever been processed. Had someone asked the mail sorter at my post office to drop it in my box, or had I picked it up from the kitchen table with the rest of the mail after putting away the groceries? Had I overlooked the letter while searching for an intruder?

I walked through the entire house a second time, not in search of someone hiding behind the bathroom door or in the hall closet, but looking for something extra, for something less. Had anything been taken? Had something else been left behind? I had never bothered with emptying my wife's closet. I'm not sure how I felt about her disappearance and death. This line might sound cruel, or maybe careless, but I wonder if I ever sat still long enough to imagine a life without my wife, even though I was already leading it. In those days, I couldn't bring myself to inspect her final note to me or to think about what Ben Miller and Sonia had told me. The story Beth recounted was off limits as well. I had stored the information, I knew where to find it, but my mind would not give me access. At odd times of the day, I would start crying only to stop abruptly after a few seconds for fear of being overwhelmed. In those brief moments I lost the ability to breathe, and something much too dark, much too sinister announced itself. I couldn't face it. Not yet, not yet.

It was only after completing my second round that I finally caught sight of them. After I had given up and was standing in the bedroom, looking at the untouched side where my wife had slept, I saw her sandals. I had registered them during my initial search, and yet I had failed to remember that she had taken them with her months earlier. They had been a gift from me; made from brown leather, the straps were studded with rhinestones, the heels impossibly high. Everything about them was garish when you really thought about it, and this had been our little joke. She'd never worn them outside, had only ever worn the sandals for me.

I didn't pick them up, and that night I chose to sleep on the couch. The dogs and the lit tree kept me company. I waited for a phone call. I waited for a knock at the door.

4

Sometimes I attempt to travel back to the sixteen-year-old listening to albums in my room after Christmas and before the New Year, a time that never was recorded, that didn't even exist. It was the time between the years, when time takes a break from moving forward and moves from corner to corner, sits down with an empty stomach and stares around. Time has unwound and it's not to be rewound until much later.

Thirty years ago, I was a week away from losing my virginity and hadn't even met the girl yet. Instead, I was exchanging love letters with a substitute teacher who had moved back north, somewhere near Marquette. Everything was possibility, nothing incurable had yet happened. I was waiting for life to begin, not realizing that I had already fallen behind. What waste, what lightness. I felt so light, for days I couldn't set foot on the sometimes wet, sometimes frozen ground beyond the house in that small Michigan town. I lived with my parents and sister, but for all true purposes, I was living alone.

I made coffee the morning after I received E. P. Holst's letter and listened to the records the sixteen-year-old had listened to, the boy who was yearning to love and to be felt, the one who couldn't wait to grow up and yet couldn't muster any decisive step toward adulthood. On good days I was in love with this indecision, the dead ends, the hurts, the small cuts, the odd scars. Some nights I was afraid to leave the world with nothing put in order.

The tree was still lit, the house still dark, though it was past ten thirty. A cold front was coming with rain moving in and out. The dogs received a ham steak each for breakfast. When I had been sixteen — and maybe this stage had lasted until I was twenty-three — books were more real than life, because the experiences I was able to obtain myself felt devoid of mystery, devoid of magic. I had lived so little, I needed books to talk about anything at all. They were manuals, maps, travel guides. They were more fulfilling than the experience of traveling myself. It was the most beautiful way of moving about the world.

The thrill of doing the "real" thing came later and proved to be painful in new, highly unpleasurable ways. It's the only way to be, really, unless you choose the existence of a monk — not a real one, an imagined one — and choose books over the kisses and bodies and the miles traveled toward some destination you don't know exists. Foreign countries, jobs, loves, apartments, accolades. Once you choose the real life, the life in which you don't dream of who you might become but the life in which you experience who you are and how other people are viewing you, you can't go back. You won't fit into your old dreams anymore.

How shabby I turned out to be.

It was the time between the years, when time forgets about us and gives us long hours to contemplate what we have become and who we used to be. Between the years, all my previous selves occupied the same space and looked at one another with suspicion, regret, or confusion. Some of my selves didn't recognize others, doubted there had ever been such versions. Some seemed polished to within an inch of their lives; all the dings and scratches had disappeared. I didn't ask for forgiveness, I'd have to confess first.

I took Natalie's sandals, placed them in a plastic bag and took them to the garage. I opened the windows of the bedroom despite the rain.

*

Detective Glasgow was at his desk when I arrived before the New Year. I dropped off the bag containing sandals and letter, though I doubted they would be of any use to him. He took and re-bagged them, left the room to send them to the lab. "I have a favor to ask," he said when he returned from his errant. "I won't get permission to fly to Cambridge and talk to the parents of the boy, and my colleagues in London are about to give up on the case."

"You are sending your prime suspect to talk to the parents."

"They might see a kindred spirit in you. You suffered the same loss."

"I'm not a wealthy man," I said. "And what if they don't want to talk about their son? What if they find the similarities between their son's case and mine merely grotesque?"

He looked at me for some time, without letting on what he was thinking. "They're expecting you on the sixth. The husband was against the idea, but Mrs. Sadeghi said she would welcome the chance to talk to you. You have no official role, you're not reporting to me, we have absolutely no ties, and we never talked about any of this."

*

The London hotel I had booked last minute turned out to be a worse fleabag than the pictures had let on. I took several Advil and went straight to bed, then woke up at four o'clock in the morning, the TV in the room next door sending gunshots and police sirens my way. Cigarette smoke inexplicably hung about my room. On my way to the bathroom, tiny bodies scuttered beyond my peripheral vision. Instead of waiting for daylight, I stepped into the streets and walked I didn't know where.

Of course I had accepted Glasgow's offer. I was certain now that he'd never had any doubts about that. The dogs I had dropped off with a neighbor, a retired teacher who'd lost his own dog a few months earlier and was happy to have company for a few days. Nobody anticipated my return.

I'd never traveled to England and was shocked by how bracing the cold was, how shabby the city looked in early January. I had lived in California for long enough to have forgotten about what weather really was. The cold drove me into a fast-food joint serving breakfast, and once the first shops started to open, I ducked into a small work-wear store and bought a heavy coat with fake fur trim and an extra thick beanie.

I hadn't wanted to face the Sadeghis tired and jet-lagged, with a raging headache and blood-shot eyes, and had arrived a day early, but during my first hours in London, I admitted to myself that my planning had been poor. I had no reason to look at St. Paul's, nor was I keen on looking at the Tower Bridge or Scotland Yard. Even if I had tried, I wouldn't have been able to enjoy London's sights. Instead, I sat in cafes and pubs for much of the day, doubting my decision to pay for such an extravagance. Natalie was dead. No searching, no visits to foreign countries could bring her back.

In the late afternoon, with the light fading quickly, I stood inside a churchyard, in front of a curious pyramidal tomb to the west of the church proper. I wasn't quite sure how I'd gotten there, what had driven me to this point, but I no longer questioned my endeavor. Maybe fatigue finally let me relax, and I went inside, removing my hat, soaking in the relative warmth of the building. A woman in her forties left a group of teenagers near the altar and strode towards me. She greeted me in a whisper, put a hand on my arm, and asked if she could help me. I only shook my head. The cold had left me stunned, my face was numb, my hands red and blue. I had never removed the golden wedding ring.

She got up on her tiptoes and brought her lips to my ear. "You found what you were looking for. You can feel it, can't you? It's quite splendid, it's all being exposed in the shadows." Her eyes nearly disappeared behind her thick glasses. Her hand gave me a final squeeze and she left as quickly as she had come.

*

When Farid's mother led me up to his room on the second floor of their house in an older development at the outskirts of town, I could sense her bewilderment. She must have been some ten years younger than me, with a rounded back and black hair that she wore in a ponytail with gray, wiry streaks running through it. I might have described her as looking bookish, but I hadn't seen a single book downstairs.

Her son's room smelled like a museum, not a single pencil lay askance, not even the roller skates at the bottom of the closet appeared to have been used, so meticulously had their wheels been cleaned.

"You came all the way from California? The police already looked through everything," she said. "What was your wife's name again?"

I told her. I had been vague about her death, had only focused on the missing feet in an attempt to create enough trust for her to open up Farid's room for me. It felt wrong, as though I were a hyena feasting on the dead, but now I was in Cambridge on the second floor of a house that smelled of coffee and carpet cleaner, and once I started talking about Natalie I couldn't stop. All the while, we stood in the small room, not moving, not touching a thing.

I had passed the time before my visit to the Sadeghis' house in a coffee shop, jotting down questions I should ask. I hadn't been able to focus on what lay ahead, not on the plane and neither in London. My head had been empty, the way I felt during the few times I had caught the flu or some other bug. I had surrendered to it, hoping to clear my mind in time for my meeting with the dead boy's mother. But even after a second mug I failed to come up with more than a few question that, on reading what I had jotted down, sounded rude and heartless, as though I had come to insult the dead.

Standing in Farid's small museum of a room, I was at a loss, and because I couldn't think of anything to ask that wasn't an abomination, I told Mrs. Sadeghi about the paper house. I hadn't planned to divulge that part — it seemed sacred and monstrous at the same time — and yet her eyes wanted me to continue. Silently she was asking me to reveal something that made sense and would help with her own grief.

No sooner had I come to the part of walking around Natalie's work and peering in at the faithful reconstructions of our belongings and furnishings, she clasped her hands and inquired about the night of the fire that had destroyed our neighborhood. I recounted how the dogs had awakened us around one in the morning, and how Natalie and I had been checking the internet for information, how a patrol car had rolled down our streets, the two cops asking us to leave just after I had extinguished a fire in my neighbor's yard. When I got to the point at which we had just grabbed our dogs and passports, Mrs. Sadeghi became animated. "You could have died," she said with something akin to enthusiasm. Her eyes lit up like two pieces of coal.

"Yes," I said. "If our dogs hadn't started to bark that night, we would have burned in our sleep."

"Our Farid nearly died when he was twelve."

It was clear that she wanted me to ask about this episode, and so I did. As though the question had broken the spell, she sat down on Farid's bed, and motioned for me to take a seat on the desk chair. "He was on a camping trip with his best friend."

"The one who accompanied him to London?" I interrupted.

Her face harshened. "Yes, Gavin. The Lowrys went up north and took our boy with them." She stopped briefly, apparently making adjustments in her mind. Her voice had sounded accusatory but softened once she continued. "They liked Farid. Everybody liked Farid. He was so serious, and he was a good student. Gavin got passing grades only because of our son. Farid would study with him nearly every day." The family had been camping at the site for many years. It lay outside a small town near Hull, not far from the coast. One night the boys ventured out by themselves without telling Gavin's parents. Armed with two flashlights they set out into the woods surrounding the campground and almost immediately got lost. Everything had looked unfamiliar at night, and no matter how hard they tried, they seemed to get farther and farther away from their tent. The weather had been moody all day, and after half an hour it started to rain. To make matters worse, a thunderstorm lit up the sky repeatedly. Drenched and scared, the boys found a way out of the forest, but they still didn't know where they were. They thought they could see a road ahead, and to get there, they climbed through a barbed wire fence into what looked to be a cow pasture. Gavin cleared the fence without difficulty, but Farid's jacket snagged on the rusty wire, and while trying to extract himself, lightning struck.

"He could have died, but he didn't. He passed out, and Gavin pulled him away from the fence and sat with him in the mud until Farid opened his eyes again. They later found that they had been only five minutes away from the campsite. The Lowrys hadn't even noticed their absence, but Gavin woke them, and they drove Farid to the emergency room. The doctors said he was very lucky."

"You must have been scared."

"When they called us, we immediately got in the car and picked him up. I was crying the whole way. He could have died." She was so caught up in the memories of that trip, that she didn't realize what she had said until a moment later. Then she sat in silence, her mouth contorting, her eyes not seeing anything.

Later, when we had left Farid's room and she offered to make some coffee, she said, "He wasn't the same after the incident. He worked so hard, and he was top of his class, but his heart wasn't in it. Even after the dizziness and the headaches subsided, I felt as though after that night when he was struck by lightning, he stopped being a boy. He stopped playing catch with Babak, and he stopped playing the piano. Instead, he would sit for hours in the backyard and stare. A teenager is not supposed to stare into the sky all afternoon, don't you agree?" She stopped for a second, then muttered, "Oh, I want to show you something." She went back upstairs, and I could hear her open drawers and doors. A few minutes later she returned with a small book. She must have seen me stare, maybe she saw something that I didn't want to reveal, because after

I had taken the book from her hand, she said in a voice which now sounded hoarse, "You found one too, didn't you? You know what this is."

I found myself in the Sadeghis' living room sometime later, not knowing how much time had passed, or when Mrs. Sadeghi had invited me to sit squeezed into the corner of an old blue sofa. Instead of coffee, a glass of whiskey was in my hand, the insidious book before me on the table. Mrs. Sadeghi sat in an armchair across from me. How long we had been drinking I had no idea. "At first, I didn't want to talk to you. I thought you were one of them," she said.

"Of them?"

"You got a visit too, didn't you? A young man came, asked for my husband. He asked if he could wait for Babak, and I offered him coffee. We sat here in the living room. He sat in the same spot you're in, but he refused the coffee. There was something wrong with him, I thought, he looked way too pale. He looked like the dead."

"What did he tell you?" I asked.

Mrs. Sadeghi took a sip of her own drink. "He said I hadn't been worth having a son. And you know, I fought it, I did, but I felt caught."

"Caught?" I repeated. It was the same word I had used to explain why I hadn't asked Beth more questions.

"Yes, I felt guilty," she continued. "What I had feared since Farid was a small boy and started to crawl away from me and discover the world without my constant help, this visitor confirmed. He had never been mine. I had been a hindrance, an impediment. I had kept him from being who he really was." She looked at me sharply, as if my mind could be read from across the table. "It's what they told you about your wife as well, isn't it? That you were a shit, unworthy of taking care of her." Mrs. Sadeghi paused for a moment. "You know, he wasn't like my Farid, not at all, but while he sat where you are sitting now, I wanted to hold him."

"Did you?" I asked.

She only stopped crying several minutes later. During that time, I noticed that I was still wearing the blue coat I had bought that morning. I should have been sweaty, I should have been warm, but I pulled the material tighter around me.

"I held him, and he held me. We sat here for hours, and I ran my hands over him, again and again, as though Farid had returned. Why did they have to paint him as though he were rotting? Why did they have to take his feet? Why did they have to do that?"

"I should go," I said once she had calmed down. "Your husband will be back."

She shook her head. "He's staying the night at a friend's cabin. He thinks I'm making things up. He thinks you're a reporter trying to get a good story. He calls me foolish."

"Have they contacted you? Have they promised to meet with you?"

"I would never," she hissed. "Those animals. I would tear out their eyes. Why? Have you talked to them?"

I shook my head. "No, sometimes I wish they would explain, but no, I haven't received or heard anything."

Mrs. Sadeghi seemed satisfied with my lie, maybe it was the most plausible explanation. How could I want to speak to the people who had killed my wife? What kind of monster was I? She asked if I had taken a picture of Natalie's paper house, and I pulled it up on my phone.

Mrs. Sadeghi took it greedily from my hand and studied the photo as though she wanted to memorize every single detail. "She captured it all," she said. "Her old life, it's all there."

*

That night I stayed up until the local donut shop across the street from my hotel opened at five. I sat at a small Formica table in front of the large, drafty window and ate the donut and slurped the scalding hot, weak coffee. Then I bought a second donut and a second coffee. After that I went back to my hotel room. The night was slowly melting, the gray becoming runny, and I was no longer afraid to sleep.

Back home, I started to work again. Routine had given me a certain speed over the years, but I had never become sloppy. Even my most banal canvases were done with care. As long as I didn't conjure Natalie's face, the way she had looked in the mornings over coffee, or Mrs. Sadeghi's look of pity and greed, I could start work before ten in the morning and stay in the garage until after eight at night. On the plane back to California, my intention had been to call Detective Glasgow right after picking up the dogs from my neighbor. On arrival in Santa Rosa, however, I couldn't remember why. Four days later I still hadn't worked up the nerve.

The whole time I was keeping busy I in my garage, I could feel the presence of the small volume I had found in Natalie's storage unit, the same that Mrs. Sadeghi had found among her son's belongings. This miserable book galled me; its short, clipped chapters and its deceitful language choked me. At first, I had left it on the coffee table, but by now I had banned it to the hall bathroom's cabinet, and I hadn't set foot in that room since. Still, I could feel it the way you can feel a migraine coming, the way you know you're not alone even though you haven't spotted the intruder yet.

One morning, after working feverishly for several hours, I stepped back from the canvas to inspect its overall effect. I'd had the entire painting in my head, I knew every inch of it, and yet, when I laid eyes on it from a few feet away, I felt suddenly weak and sank onto a stool. The painting in my head was not what I had done to the canvas. Rather, I was now looking at a rendering of Natalie's paper house. The front door stood open, and I could see the blue sofa in the living room and the painting of a house we'd once bought in Los Angeles above it. A round green coffee table held a few magazines.

I closed my eyes like a child, trying to unsee the disaster I had created. On opening them again, the canvas hadn't changed. No matter what I had set out to paint, I had merely recreated Natalie's work.

The following day I had no better luck. Again, I studied my sketches before setting out to work, and for the first few hours I meant to accomplish the set task. But after four in the afternoon, after I had exhausted myself and took a break to view what I had done, the canvas again showed Natalie's paper house, this time the view through her office's open window. Her desk was there, her small, fanciful lamps, an open closet full of clothes and shoes.

From then on, my work slowed, my work hours shrank. I drank more, started on the bourbon in the early afternoon hours. Several times I thought about calling Farid's mother to inquire about what powers the book held over her, yet each time I looked at my phone, I called myself a coward. I called myself superstitious, weak, needy, and neurotic. I began yelling at myself.

*

The fire started on the second try. The dogs weren't used to the beach at night and stayed close, whining softly. I hadn't dared strike a match in my backyard, because even keeping a small fire pit or a charcoal grill seemed unthinkable in a neighborhood that had been razed by wildfire. Instead, I had made the drive out to Schoolhouse Beach. No one else was near the water, and the cliffs protected me from view of people driving past on the highway. The dogs had never showed any fear of fire, but this time they avoided the flames and started to growl and bark and put up their mohawks once I took the book from my bag and threw it onto the pile of dry wood. They pulled at their leashes, tried to drag me away. Yet I made sure the pages had burned completely before I left. I heaped sand on top of the ashes and placed rocks on top of the sand. Nobody must ever find a single shred of the insidious volume.

Day after day I set out to work on canvases I could sell. Day after day I failed. In the end I had to admit that the exorcism had destroyed the book but done nothing to lessen its power. Every painting I finished only showed another detail of Natalie's paper house; I couldn't escape its pull. After two weeks of fruitless effort, I finally grew so exhausted that I stopped painting altogether. I locked the garage and spent the waking hours watching reruns of old television shows, the more lurid and ludicrous the better. I was afraid of Natalie's creation, and even more afraid of my own work. At night, before falling asleep, I made plans to sell the house.

*

At the end of January, on a bright and cold morning, Glasgow paid me a visit. I had just fed the dogs and was wearing sweats and a hoodie when he rang the doorbell. I felt guilty for never reporting what I had found out on my trip to Cambridge, but he didn't seem to pay much attention to my excuses, barely listened to my hurried account of visiting Mrs. Sadeghi. After I had made coffee and opened a package of biscotti, and after we sat down at the kitchen table, he finally let me know why he had wanted to see me. "Craig didn't call you?" he asked, but my face must have told him that I had no idea why he was asking. He lowered his voice and spoke to his coffee mug, not looking my way. Sonia had been found in her bathtub, three empty pill bottles on the tiled floor below.

My hands started to tremble so violently that I had to set down the cup. Coffee spilled onto the table, and I hastily got up and looked for a towel. I opened cabinet after cabinet like an idiot, as though I had never lived in this house, had never looked at the contents before. When I finally pulled open the right drawer, I nearly cried I was so happy to grab a towel and dab at the spilled liquid. "Did you find a note?" I asked.

Glasgow shook his head. "But her husband seems to believe that you and Natalie, but mostly you, are to blame for her death. He says you visited their house after your wife's disappearance, and that she spurred his advice and visited you once we had recovered the body."

"Craig blamed me?" My voice sounded incredibly thin.

"He thinks you blamed his wife for Natalie's death, and that you wanted to destroy her as well."

"Because he thinks I destroyed Natalie?"

Glasgow dunked a biscotti in his cup. "I think you believe that too."

"But not in the way he sees it. It's not a simple cause-and-effect affair. I never beat Natalie, I never abused her. I hardly ever raised my voice. I think we were quite happy for a long time. But once you get married, love becomes a savage. It savages most couples."

"About Cambridge..."

This time I took time to get the details right. I told Glasgow what I had learned, mentioned even that Farid had been struck by lightning. "His mother seemed to link that episode to us losing our house in the fire. We could have died; Farid could have died back then."

The detective emptied his cup, which I carried to the kitchen for a refill. He didn't say anything until I had put the fresh coffee in front of him. He added three spoonfuls of sugar and asked, "Do you believe there is such a link?"

"If both my wife and Farid were killed by the same person, a sense of loss might have driven them to seek solace, to look for help. Still, a seventeen-year-old high schooler and a forty-seven-year-old woman hardly share the same world view or the same sensibilities."

Glasgow appraised me for a long time. "Maybe you're right." He drew out his words until his statement suggested the opposite. "Did you find anything else in the storage unit? You know I will have to take a look."

I shook my head.

"Nothing out of the ordinary?"

"The paper house isn't strange enough?" On a sudden whim I asked, "Did Farid leave behind anything unusual? I was in his room. It looked like a regular boy's room. Maybe too clean, too orderly, but that might be due to Mrs. Sadeghi. But did Farid do anything...peculiar?"

Glasgow frowned. Then he asked for a piece of paper and scribbled down a URL. "This will answer your question. And I would refrain from contacting Sonia's husband. If he appears at your door, pretend you're not home."

For a long time after he'd shut the door behind him, I sat at the table, staring out onto the backyard where Tonda chased after birds and Anemone sat in the shade of the tool shed. Finally, I opened my laptop and typed in the web address Glasgow had given me. Initially, what I saw didn't seem to make sense. The site contained a choose-your-own-adventure game called "It Was a Dark and Stormy Night." But once I clicked through the first pages, the hero, a badly drawn teenager called Farid, made his entrance. He and his friend Gavin are going on a camping trip with Gavin's parents. One night they leave their tent to walk alone in the storm.

I played the game the rest of the morning and all afternoon. There were four different paths a player could take after leaving the tent, and each of the paths branched out into four more paths, and so on. The drawings weren't sophisticated, the backgrounds had been culled from other websites. By nine in the evening, I had played through fifty different paths. In some, the boys, after getting lost, traced their steps back to the campsite. In others, they followed a creek, swollen with rainwater, until they came to a lake. Others still saw them arrive in a small village. But all the different pathways had one thing in common. At the end, Farid was hit by lightning and died.

"How did you find it?" I texted Glasgow.

The answer didn't even take a minute to arrive. "The other boy, Gavin."

I looked at the screen of my laptop again, where Farid still lay without moving. There were at least two-hundred paths left to explore. Why, why had I not told Glasgow about the book? Why didn't I tell him now? What kept me from revealing its existence?

<h1 style="text-align:center">5</h1>

The letter arrived two days later. February was announcing itself with heavy rains. I didn't recognize the handwriting, the finely curled letters, the crooked lines which my wet hand hands threatened to render illegible. I had never before received a note from Sonia.

The envelope contained four pages and a photograph. In the picture, Sonia and Natalie stood on a beach I had never seen before. It was black, fog covering most of the hills beyond. It seemed that Sonia had held the camera, and her face was smiling, though there was something jarring about her serious or even anxious eyes and her toothy grin. Next to her, Natalie didn't smile, and neither did she look unhappy or worried. There was something very serene about her features; maybe she was scared.

"I wasn't quite honest with you," the letter began. "What I said was true, but I didn't tell you everything. I was too confused and afraid of the consequences." A few weeks after Natalie had taken the picture of Ursa Carmel's brochure, she had surprised her friend by suggesting a trip up north to Shelter Cove. By then, she had already left me to live in a motel and told Sonia she was looking for "something permanent." They agreed to take Sonia's car and during the drive, Natalie explained that she was going to meet Ursa Carmel in Shelter Cove, that everything had been arranged.

"She said it was the book. The book had led her to accept that she needed to see the healer and become whole again. What she said in the car was that she couldn't be "this person" anymore. I didn't know what exactly she meant. I thought she was referring to you and being married to you."

The last two sentences had been crossed out but were still legible. Sonia had added, "I thought she meant being married and living a life of routine."

In Shelter Cove, the two women stayed in a house by the water. Sonia felt nervous, something felt off about Natalie. Her friend seemed too calm, always in thought. It was hard to get her to talk about what she expected from meeting the healer. And Sonia grew worried because they didn't even know what the healer looked like. Anybody could assume her role.

"On the second day, we both went to see her at an address Nat had been given. The house stood in a wooded area, not far from the beach, but when we entered, all the rooms were empty, as though nobody had been living there for quite some time. The woman who called herself Ursa took me by the arm and dragged me outside. I wasn't allowed to stay, I wasn't even allowed to wait for Nat. She said, 'Your role ends today. You can't be of any use to your friend.'"

Sonia was hurt by Ursa's harsh words, but Natalie didn't come to her defense. She didn't even say goodbye. Sonia waited in their rented house all night, but Natalie never returned. They had arrived on a Tuesday; on Friday their lease was up, and Sonia left in Natalie's car, with her friend's bag in the trunk. After Natalie had been found dead, she threw everything away. She blamed herself for her friend's death and was afraid the police might find out about the trip.

"But I'm more afraid of *them*. I am more afraid of the book that led Natalie to them. I know that it was the book that made her go to Shelter Cove. I should have died there too."

After reading the letter a second time, I returned to the picture, studying every inch of the 8x10 print. I believe it must have been Natalie's solemn expression that kept me from looking beyond the two women to a much smaller figure standing farther down the beach. I couldn't tell whether that figure was male or female, nor how old this person might be. Black clothes revealed nothing but very white hands. I thought the person's face was turned away from the women, because I couldn't make out any features, but once I had located my old magnifying glass, I saw that the figure in black had drawn a hood over their head. As far as I could tell, a mask covered their mouth, the same kind I had used every day during the worst of the pandemic. Frustrated, I put down magnifying glass and photo. What I had learned seemed important, but what more did I really know? Who had given Natalie the small volume? And how had it led her to the Flamingo and, finally, Shelter Cove? After reading Sonia's letter, how much more did I really understand?

*

I didn't contact Craig, though at times it seemed the reasonable, the compassionate thing to do. Hadn't we once been friends? Hadn't we both lost our wives? Yet whatever had happened in Shelter Cove, could reason even start to explain it? Were the deaths of Natalie and Sonia occurrences reason could wrap its mind around?

Sonia was buried one rainy Friday, and I knew better than to make the short trip to Rohnert Park. Rather than causing a scene at the funeral, I sat on the patio, an occasional gust of wind whipping water into my face. I had stopped working early that morning, and the feeling that I was a stranger in my own life and house only intensified. My mind and my hands refused to work together; what I painted was no longer what I imagined, but what stalked me once I closed my eyes at night. After ruining yet another canvas, I had decided to give up and finally contacted a realtor I knew. Around noon, while Sonia's casket was lowered into the ground, she walked with me through the house, making suggestions on how to stage the individual rooms. She was discreet, she knew enough about Natalie's story not to ask any questions.

I went to work on small repairs, I boxed up the belongings that weren't presentable, and tried to rearrange the rest to suggest that this had been a happy home. Danielle, the realtor, helped from time to time and even hung new curtains. She hired a gardener to take care of my overgrown backyard. After three weeks' time, the house looked like a credible impression of a home — I had exorcised my own presence. During our last walk-through, she took down the only remaining picture of Natalie that I hadn't yet boxed. "Your name will of course be on all the documents, but you don't want buyers to look you up on the internet. You could leave a lot of money on the table if they saw a photo of you or your wife. Don't leave any mail where they can find it. If I were you, I'd move to a hotel until this is done." She smiled, embarrassed maybe that she had to explain.

*

The detective arrived twenty minutes late in Sebastopol; the morning rain was just about to stop. During my childhood in Michigan, February had been the most dreadful month; here, it meant the surrounding hills were teeming with green. It meant you could once again wear sandals and leave the patio open all day.

"I'll be careful," Glasgow assured me. After I opened the gate to reveal the paper house, he took several steps back. For a minute or two he looked away, down the miserable alley of this storage facility. Without turning to face me, he said, "A friend of mine gave me a puzzle for Christmas, five-hundred pieces. I started it right away, you know, I wanted to show him my appreciation."

"You did?"

Glasgow didn't show whether he'd heard me or not, didn't even pause. "So far, I might have assembled fifty or eighty pieces max."

"What are you saying?"

"Was your wife always this driven?"

She hadn't been. Natalie had often joked that she was born for retirement. Feverish work, long nights spent on pet projects, the ambition to excel at any cost — none of these things had interested her. She had kept the temperature of her pursuits low. "I never got to know the woman who did this," I said.

Glasgow walked around the structure, peeking through the windows and open doors. "What do you make of it?" he asked.

I had no answer for him, no conclusion, even though I had spent much time in its presence. "She didn't even like the old house much. We bought it because it had most everything we needed or wanted, but mainly because it was available and we could afford it."

"You could have died in the fire," he said.

"Those are Mrs. Sadeghi words. You think Farid's website and this house are born from the same impulse?"

He shrugged. "The work consumed both of them, no matter how you look at it. Maybe there was something your wife didn't want to forget. Or something she wanted to return to. Did you find something unusual?"

I told him I hadn't. Again, I kept quiet about *The Nine Thoughts*, though I still couldn't say why. Like an inappropriate attachment, I guarded it with suspicion and anxiety. Glasgow took a painting off the wall and checked its backside. He lifted books and magazines off the coffee table and inspected them. "Is there something that doesn't fit?"

"This is not *Sesame Street*," I snapped.

"But you must have asked yourself what it means. Especially since she kept it hidden from you. What was she trying to remember or recreate? If you're right and she didn't love the house?"

Later, he took a brief look at the other storage unit, but after I assured him that the items were not replicas of our old furniture, he quickly lost interest, and we returned to the paper house. He sat down on the workbench in silence. The rain had returned and picked up its clattering and clinking, occasionally broke into a wild pounding of the roof. I took a seat on a chair in front of the entrance to the paper house; Glasgow's presence made me uncomfortable; he didn't belong.

"She's here, right?" he said into my thoughts. "I might be diluting the experience, but she's here?"

"How do you mean?"

"It feels like a portal, doesn't it? You're here now, and I think she's here too, somehow."

"A portal?" I echoed.

He stretched out his hand in front of him as though he might be able to lift up the house and turn it this way and that to make me see what he felt. "If you keep looking hard enough, your wife will appear and join you. I mean, I can see who you were, I feel I know what kind of life you were leading. In your new house, I don't know; in your new house, you can't feel her presence at all, even though she left most of her things behind, you say."

As if the skies above wanted to chime in, thunder became audible. We both looked up — it hardly ever thunders in Northern California. We waited for lightning, waited for another rumbling. But Glasgow was right, most of all, we were waiting for Natalie to appear inside the house, step through the open door and confide in us.

*

As it turned out, there was no need for me to check into a hotel. Things sorted themselves out in much different ways, though by then I had come to expect them. A day after Danielle put the house on the market, I received a call from Glasgow. Two hours later I once again dropped off the dogs at my neighbor's house. Three hours after that, I sat on a plane to Dallas with a connecting flight to Tampa, Florida.

It was night by the time I arrived, the humidity hitting me with a force I hadn't anticipated. I sat in the back of the cab with the windows lowered. Whatever the AC put out in front was lost on me. My shirt responded audibly whenever I tore myself away from the seat and leaned forward to answer the drivers' insistent questions about where I was from and what I was going to do in his city, and again when I was finally allowed to step outside and into the entrance area of the hotel.

The bartender was already packing up but agreed to sell me a bottle of bourbon and a bowl of nuts. In California it was only 8:30, so I sat on the balcony of my room and looked out onto the river, people strolling and biking along a paved walkway. It was still warm enough to wear nothing but boxers. I listened to the voices reaching me from the pool area until I was drunk enough to sleep.

*

The drive to St. Pete was short, the address I had typed into my phone situated on a quiet street near the water. The one-story house appeared well-kept, friendly. A large screened-in porch ran along its front. Five minutes later, I sat across from a man in his fifties, with a goatee, thinning hair, and a bit of a belly. After he pulled open the door, we stared at each other a few seconds too long — the similarities of our build and appearance, from our height and weight to our all-black clothes, seemed uncanny. Then he said, "Well, come in, Mr. Doppelganger."

Glasgow had announced and vouched for me. He was using me, though I wasn't sure exactly how. Couldn't he just have made a call? What did he hope this man might reveal to me that he wouldn't tell the police? Nathan was his name. His husband Kurt had been found in a New Orleans hotel three years prior, his body painted to look diseased and putrefied, his feet missing. "He should have been in Pensacola with his sister. He had been staying with her for a few days. She has a boat out there. They were going to scatter the ashes of their old man. He was a piece of shit, but for some reason they wanted to go ahead with this ceremony. Maybe they just wanted to feed him to the fish and make sure he couldn't come back." He made a whistling noise. "But the morning they were supposed to head out, Kurt was gone. Simply gone, though most of his stuff was still in the guest room."

"Did she find a brochure? Have you found the brochure of a healer?"

"Not exactly." He stretched the words, maybe wondering what I was after. "But he left her a note written on this." He reached for something on a small shelf and handed it to me. It was a glossy postcard art galleries and theaters use to advertise their upcoming shows. The backside was entirely empty and white, and Kurt had written, "Don't worry. I'm heading out and may be some time." The front showed the picture of a man standing in an open field. Behind him, in the distance, another man was raising his arms, as if to warn the first of some imminent threat. But on closer inspection, the two men were the same. The words printed below the image read, "Time to Head Back."

On an impulse, I asked if he could give me a tour of the house. Nathan seemed taken aback, but then said, "Yeah, why not." Again, I had this awkward feeling of meeting myself while we stood facing each other, as though I might be staring at my reflection. "Weird, huh?" Nathan said and grinned. "You know, unless I'm in the bathroom and shaving or brushing my teeth, I don't realize how much I have aged. In my mind I'm maybe thirty. Thirty-five tops."

I nodded. "But when you look at me, you know. You *understand*."

"Yes," he said. "Shame."

Most of the furniture was dark wood, the color of the walls eggshell. Shelves and tables had an antique look about them, and there were knickknacks everywhere, though not of the cheap kind. All objects, from wall clocks to bookends, from napkin holders to a brass kitchen scale, were exquisite. And each item had found its one correct spot in the house, it seemed. Everything appeared utterly harmonious. "I haven't changed a thing since his death," Nathan said. "My way of keeping him around."

Something I couldn't have foreseen awaited me in what he announced had been Kurt's study. Above a black leather couch hung one of my paintings, an older one in a style I had long abandoned. It was from a time when I had still tried to make it big and take the art world by storm.

Nathan must have caught me staring; my expression must have been utterly idiotic. "Something wrong?"

I shook my head, pointed at the canvas, but couldn't speak.

"You look like you've seen a ghost."

I stepped closer to the painting. Yes, yes, I was seeing a ghost. There she was, at the bottom of the canvas, Natalie, her figure barely visible among dark, bare trees. The painting was held in black and white, though a sepia tone had crept in at the end. The composition felt abstract, maybe a harbinger of things to come, but there she was, blurry and naked. Natalie.

"He got that at an estate sale. You okay?"

I nodded, told him I had painted it nearly twenty years prior. This made Nathan join me in front of the canvas and he looked at the signature in the righthand corner. "Fuck," he said. "That's you. I'm really sorry, but I told Kurt not to get it. I mean, it looks very much the way the old one looked. It's pretty too, beautiful really, but it has always unsettled me. Something's wrong in that picture. I'm sorry, I really am. I'm not trying to talk shit about your work."

I wasn't offended. His words pulled me out of my helplessness. "The way the old one looked?"

He grinned broadly, exposing long, slightly stained teeth. "This isn't our first home."

"Not your first?" I repeated.

"We used to live in Panama City. Kurt was a teacher there." It felt as though he wanted to go on. He had already opened his lips to continue, but then he swallowed whatever it was he had intended to say.

"And the other painting didn't disturb you? What happened to it?"

Nathan stared at me expressionless for a few moments, then closed his eyes, exhaled, and said, "Seven years ago, a hurricane came through and just flattened our house. There was nothing left, plain nothing. The neighborhood looked as though garbage had been flung onto a flat field. Trees were gone, houses were gone. Kurt was big into family, he has aunts and cousins up and down the state, so he didn't want to leave Florida, but we didn't want to stay in that area."

These sentences were spoken in haste, and he was out of breath soon enough. I nodded, signaling that he should continue, and following a brief moment of silence, he did. After the storm, he and Kurt had looked for new jobs, and Nathan had found work with the city of Tampa. "Kurt was obsessed with the idea of finding a house with the exact same layout as our old one. He researched which architect had built our old home — architect my ass, just some big contractor with five floor plans — and that was a dead end. The company had never built a thing around here. Still, he made us stay in a moldy rental for two years until he found this house. It's not a perfect replica, but close. Very close. I guess most houses are not that different, give or take, but here even the front door is in the right spot. The detached garage is spot on. The house, when Kurt first showed it to me, even *felt* like the old one."

After moving in, Kurt had insisted that they find exact matches for the pieces of furniture they had lost. He bought the same appliances, curtains, linens, and waste bins. "He went nuts," Nathan said. "Sometimes I felt like I was entering a museum, at others, it was as though I was back in Panama City and our house had never been blown to bits. Some days it was soothing, others just eerie."

"What did he think?"

"I'm still not sure, and now I won't be able to ask him anymore. The search for the house and everything in it seemed to give him purpose. Every weekend he left early to hit yard and garage sales. He became friends with every antique dealer. Still, I'm not sure he was happy." Nathan paused for a moment. "We didn't spend much time together after the storm. It might sound weird, but I felt as though I might have been just another object he thought he needed for this place. He deposited me here, but he had little use for me."

I didn't answer him right away. I could hear him, I understood him, but I couldn't stop looking at Natalie in the picture above Kurt's sofa. Before this day, I had long forgotten the painting ever existed. All the photos of my work I used to own had burned in the fire. Slides and sales records had been burned as well. "She had no use for me either," I said after a while, and explained how I had insisted on only buying things that bore little resemblance to what we had lost. I told Nathan what Glasgow had only sketched out for him. The fire, her disappearance, my trip to Reno, the paper house. "At times I'm not sure I have much use for myself. What is it about my painting that unnerves you?"

"As I said, the old one was similar, the same colors, or lack of colors, really. But it feels — please don't laugh — like an obituary. No, that's not it. As though a death is being announced before it has happened. I'm sorry, I might just be projecting my own fear onto your painting." He led us back to the living room and got two bottles of beer from the refrigerator. "A bit early, but fuck it," he said and placed one in front of me. "Kurt is not the first one, then?"

I shook my head, filled him in on Mrs. Sadeghi's son.

"So why isn't it all over the news?" he asked.

"You can find each individual case if you know what you're looking for. But the police aren't releasing all the information, and..." I drifted off.

"You had a visitor after Kurt's death."

Nathan nodded. "Not my finest hour. I should have thrown the bastard out. First he tells me how Kurt would have left me anyway, then he tries to charm me."

"Did he succeed?"

"As I said, not my finest hour."

"Where is it?" I asked.

He didn't ask me what I meant, just stood up and walked toward the back of the house, then returned carrying the small volume and put it on the table in front of me. "I haven't talked to anyone about it. Not the police, not even a friend. I've been on medical leave since Kurt's death, my doctor renews his evaluation every six months without asking. Sometimes I think Kurt was selfish not to take me with him."

"Has anybody contacted you after...after what wasn't your finest hour?"

He shook his head. "I'd kill them. I know I would. Sometimes I feel that they not only took Kurt but also my dignity. As though they set out to prove I was the bastard they claimed I was."

We drank in silence for several minutes. Then a clock chimed somewhere, and another answered from the kitchen. I asked him what he had been doing for the city.

"I'm an acoustic engineer. Not the cool kind, I'm not recording famous artists. I don't have an ear for that. I'm the kind who works on noise reduction along highways and in government buildings. It's certainly not glamorous, but it pays." He went to the kitchen and got two more bottles for us. "I'm a bit embarrassed to talk about this, but since you made the trip and we'll never see each other again, I'd like to run something by you."

"Something embarrassing?"

"You saw your wife, right? After she died? She look unharmed?"

I nodded. What was he after?

"I didn't understand everything the doctor told me, won't try to pretend. But some of Kurt's organs had burst. Organs just don't burst for no reason. But I've seen the damage sound can cause. Hell, my eardrums burst on a job when I was twenty-six. Have worn these ever since." He extracted a hearing aid from his left ear and held it up. "Without them, I wouldn't be able to have a conversation with you. They are getting smaller every year, thank God."

My face must have given me away. Nathan sank back into the sofa and re-inserted the hearing aid. He sighed and shook his head in frustration, then rubbed his hands on his pant legs. "I know I can't prove a thing, and I know it seems ridiculous. But sound can kill you in a number of ways. From 150 decibel on, sounds can start affecting your inner ear and then your inner organs. They can cause life-threatening internal injuries. Sounds above 185 decibel can impact your inner organs and cause death. They can do this by causing an air embolism in your lungs, affect inner organs, or even make your lungs explode."

"But wouldn't that take a while?" I asked. "And who would submit voluntarily to sounds like that?"

"At 185, yes, it wouldn't be quick. But if you turn it up to 240 decibel, you can get killed instantly. However, 240 decibel is hard to come by."

"You think Kurt was killed that way?"

Nathan looked at me in a peculiar way. Maybe he was afraid I would laugh at his theory, or maybe he simply didn't trust this stranger who looked like him, had lost a partner like him, and now questioned his credibility. Maybe he had decided he had little use for me. He took a sip of his beer. "Just listen. Call me nuts later. But really, what is so crazy about what I'm saying? The love of my life was killed, his feet chopped off, and his body was painted as though he had been rotting away for weeks. Then I find this book in my house, and now you're sitting in Kurt's spot, and your wife died the exact same way Kurt did. We were both visited by people afterwards to...console us? Shut us up? Make us doubt ourselves? Compared to all that, sound damage doesn't feel that crazy.

"Certain infrasound frequencies can be potentially lethal," he continued. "You can read up on that later, it's not hard to find. In the case of sounds we cannot hear, which are below or above the human frequency range, things get kind of complicated. Humans cannot hear sounds below 20 Hz or above 20,000 Hz because when sound waves travel too slowly or too quickly, our body can't translate that motion into signals our brains understand. It is entirely possible for a sound to be extremely loud and for you not to hear it but be affected by it. The low pitch sounds in particular can travel much farther than higher frequencies and affect how we feel or even kill us."

I grunted, I wanted him to continue, but a sudden thought made me interrupt him, "Are there any acoustic weapons? Are you saying Kurt was attacked by some kind of sound cannon?"

Nathan's mouth stood open for a second before he started to laugh. "No, not a cannon exactly. Although the Germans did have a *Luftkanone* in WWII. It was supposed to shoot down enemy aircraft using a vortex of sound, but they never made it work reliably. The only acoustic weapon I know of is the Long-Range Acoustic Device. Nowadays it is used for crowd control. But I've heard that the military is trying to develop sonic bullets, grenades, and even mines. Some of them supposedly use infrasound. Those are the ones I'm interested in."

"I don't follow," I admitted. "If these were common, wouldn't we read more about them?"

"Have you heard of the Havana Syndrome?"

"I thought that doctors agreed it was stress, most likely," I said.

"Yes, some say it was, but the symptoms seem too specific and long-lasting. And don't forget that acoustic weapons are not in just any doctor's arsenal. You look like a normal guy, but you don't seem to believe a word I'm saying. I do sound crazy to you, right? Doctors aren't any different. They thought fibromyalgia was a hoax. They thought burn pits in Afghanistan weren't a big deal."

I got up from the sofa and asked if I could use the bathroom. A few second later, I had locked the door behind me. I looked at the reflection in the mirror — the half-bath was so small you couldn't avoid the gilded mirror unless you were sitting down — and wondered what Detective Glasgow would have made of all of this. What would he have said had he seen Nathan and I around the coffee table? Would he have thought us brothers? And would he have scoffed at sound cannons and sound grenades? Would he have believed a word?

When I got back to the living room, Nathan stood in front of the stove in the kitchen. "I'm getting hungry," he said. "I was kind of nervous about you coming and asking a lot of stupid questions, I didn't have any breakfast this morning. I'll make enough for two, if you're interested."

I pulled a chair and sat at the kitchen table, watching Nathan fry potatoes and onions, then adding kimchi and tomatoes and beef. In a second pan, he fried four eggs. Within five or ten minutes, he'd put a heaped, steaming plate in front of me. "Nothing special but comforting."

I hadn't noticed how hungry I was. Chewing and swallowing, I could feel some of the despair that had threatened to overwhelm me dissipate. Between bites, I asked, "How much of this is science fiction?"

If I had offended him, Nathan didn't let on. "None of it, though people don't discuss this shit. I mean, it's not on NPR a lot. As soon as some doctors said it was related to stress, the whole debate around Havana Syndrome died off. Back in the fifties, some French guy, something with a "G," Garraud maybe, he was looking into low-frequency sound to create an acoustic weapon for the French military. It nearly caused the death of his researchers and himself because it made their hearts, lungs, and stomachs vibrate so hard, and the project was never completed. He had stumbled upon it by accident. The guys in his lab were experiencing bouts of overwhelming nausea. After weeks of speculation on the source of the nausea they discovered that the sound coming from one motor was so low in pitch that it was below their biological ability to hear, and that their recording equipment was not capable of detecting these frequencies. Nobody had conceived that sound might exist at such low frequencies, and so no equipment had been developed to detect it. They had looked for leaks, toxins, chemicals, what have you, but it was the sound that made them sick.

"The cause was low-frequency sound, which seems ridiculous. How can sound bring on sickness or even death? But your body reacts to sound, a train or plane passing by, the rumbling of a generator or excavator. Standing too close to speakers can cause your body to shudder." He paused briefly before asking, "Want some coffee to wash it down? I know, I know, coffee and beer, but screw it."

I said I would join him. It was nearly two in the afternoon. The world seemed to have changed in the past few hours; I felt the urge to up and leave, to run until my lungs were burning. "Still sounds far-fetched."

"But only because you haven't paid attention to any of this. In college, every single one of my professors knew about the French sound experiments. We thought it was weird shit, and they loved our incredulous stares. Got a kick out of them every time." He turned away from the coffeemaker to face me. "Consider the analogy of light from the sun. You can't see past the ultraviolet part of the spectrum, yet it can burn skin, produce skin cancers, and X-rays and gamma rays can kill. And have you gone to a live concert and felt nauseous afterwards? I went to see Pearl Jam several times in the 90s. My ears would ring for days, and once I had to throw up even though I was the designated driver and hadn't been drinking."

After placing a mug in front of me and asking if I took milk, he said, "You might have heard a church pipe organ. You might have experienced sensations of sorrow, coldness, anxiety and even shivers down the spine, and thought that was some god or some really good music, but it's the sounds we don't hear that produce the effect." He paused to take a sip of coffee himself, then laughed silently. "Now comes the really weird shit. Sounds around 19 hz match the resonant frequency of the human eyeball, and people affected by that frequency claim to have seen apparitions. In plain language, at that frequency you start seeing ghosts. The most dangerous frequency, however, is at the median alpha-rhythm frequencies of the brain, 7 hz. This is also the resonant frequency of the body's organs. At high volumes, infrasound can directly affect the human central nervous system. No more shudders. What you feel is anxiety, panic, bowel spasms, nausea, vomiting, and eventually organ rupture, even death from prolonged exposure.

"I know this sounds nuts, but what else would have ruptured Kurt's organs without causing any other damage? The police don't want to investigate it. They haven't found fingerprints or DNA on his body, they haven't found his feet. When I tried to tell them about infrasound and experiments conducted in 1950s France, their eyes just glazed over."

We moved from the kitchen to the screened-in porch. For what seemed like half an hour we didn't speak. He was silently begging me to buy into his theory, and he was expecting a decision before I left his house, the house that Kurt had meticulously furnished to look exactly like the home they'd lost. At last I asked, "What do you make of the book?"

Nathan looked at me for some time. "What do *you* make of it? You're asking a lot of questions but you're not saying much."

"I burned the copy I found among Natalie's things. A friend of my wife says Natalie found it, but that it belongs to 'them.' She committed suicide a few weeks ago."

"Fuck." He looked away, checked for the second or third time if his mug was really empty.

"It has poisoned me," I said. "How? I don't know. But I can't find solace in being alive. I am alive, I should be grateful to be alive, but the things I know don't mean the same thing as before. It's not because I miss Natalie, it's not even because her friend took her own life. It's deeper than that. It's like when you discover St. Nick is a fraud and that there's no Easter Bunny. But it feels worse, since I'm going to be fifty and thought I knew the world. All I can see and feel is the *change.* I can hear the parts humming, I can hear the machinery. If this were a movie, I'd only be hearing the whir of the projector. But I can't see or believe the projection. I see every single image, one after the other, without the ability to connect them. There is no movie."

"Did you tell the detective?" Nathan said. "But I get it. Ever since I read the book, I have started to lose my memories of Kurt. The way he moved, the way his voice sounded. I can only come up with fragments, and I don't feel a thing. It's as though he's dying a second time within me. I'm erasing him. I'm erasing my love for him, and I can't stop that process. I should be shocked and outraged by how he was found and how he was taken away from me, but here I am talking to you about *luftkanonen* and infrasound, and really, who gives a shit when none of it can make me find him again? Do you believe in an afterlife?"

I said I didn't. At some point I had sided with Zen Buddhism and given up on eternity.

"I think I understand. It's a very clear, clean belief, very attractive. I don't think I ever thought much about the afterlife, but now I hope there will be one. Let it be noisy or fiery hot or empty. I want there to be an afterlife, some form of afterlife, so Kurt can find me again. If I stay here any longer, here in St. Pete, in Florida, on this planet, I don't know, I think I will forget him. Maybe that's why this bastard came to see me after Kurt's death, maybe that's why I found this book. Sorry, I know I'm full of crap, but I will forget him, he's already being scratched out every single day, more and more. I want there to be an afterlife, I need there to be an afterlife, and I need Kurt to find me and make me remember. I want him to be there and breathe into my ear and hold me, and I don't give a flying fuck how dark and horrible this afterlife might be. Just let Kurt find me once more."

*

On the flight back to California I kept my laptop open and searched for evidence of what Nathan had told me. He had been right about everything. The French scientist Vladimir Gavreau, the experiments to weaponize sound, the burst human organs.

A psychologist at the University of Hertfordshire had suggested that the odd sensations that people attribute to ghosts may be caused by infrasonic vibrations. A lecturer in the school of international studies and law at Coventry University had written a paper some twenty years earlier, called "Ghosts in the Machine." The research found that an infrasonic signal of 19 Hz might be responsible for some ghost sightings. The lecturer had been alone one night in a supposedly haunted laboratory at Warwick, when he felt very anxious and could detect a grey blob out of the corner of his eye. When Tandy turned to face the grey blob, there was nothing.

The next day, he was working on his fencing foil, with the handle held in a vice. Although there was nothing touching it, the blade started to vibrate wildly. Further investigation led the man to discover that the extractor fan in the lab was emitting a frequency of 18.98 Hz, very close to the resonant frequency of the eye. This led the researcher to believe that the ghostly figure he'd seen was an optical illusion caused by his eyeballs resonating.

I was excited by what seemed to me a new world. I devoured article after article, but once I had landed in San Francisco, daylight as merciless as a registered nurse, I had to admit that what Nathan had told me didn't help me understand why my wife had been found dead in a hotel room, missing her feet. How his theory could explain Natalie's death I couldn't imagine.

*

My realtor Danielle had good news for me. Several offers had been made above asking price — I stood to make a significant amount of money. The buyer was paying in cash, so I wouldn't need to wait long for the closing. The days that followed I spent loading some of my prized possessions into the car and driving them to Sebastopol. There was enough room in the smaller unit Natalie had rented to hold what I didn't want to part with. I looked with jealousy at the items she had bought in preparation for leaving our marriage, and still, I didn't have the heart to throw them out. What would she have made of my intrusion?

The more time I spent inside the storage unit, the less sense her death made. She hadn't wanted to die, I told myself. A person who is buying items for a new life isn't planning on getting killed. On the last day, however, I finally opened the larger unit. The paper house stood unchanged. The discovery of its very existence had overwhelmed me the first time I had seen it, but now I was able to feel its subtler effects on me. There was a finality to its presence I had overlooked the first time. The scope and craft of the installation were astounding — more so because the artist had been living with me at the time, shared the same bed and most meals with me. And Glasgow was right — the paper house felt more alive than her collection of chairs, tables, and carpets, as though Natalie might enter through the patio door any moment now. This was a replica of what I had known, and it felt more substantial than the house we had rebuilt together and everything I had bought since the fire. The new house meant very little and tomorrow I would hand in my keys and never return; not once had I doubted my decision to sell it.

The more time I spent inside the unit, the clearer it became to me that the paper house was indeed an entrance, what Glasgow had called a portal. How I might pass through it and where it might lead I couldn't say. I meant to smell Natalie's perfume, I meant to hear her steps in the hallway. Her feet, why had they taken her feet?

6

It took me several wrong turns before I found Dr. Aloisio's office. I hadn't bothered to consult a map before approaching the large complex in San Francisco's Parnassus Heights neighborhood, and when I had finally located the right entrance to the right building, I still found the layout so confusing that I had to stop and ask for directions more than once.

Even before we shook hands, I felt an immediate aversion toward the professor. I cannot say why his features appeared so unpleasant to me, why I found his mannerisms and his low voice revolting. His face, in my agitated state, appeared as though I was viewing it through a spyhole — impossibly distorted, bulbous, bloated even. I sensed contempt when he offered me a chair; his lips were wet and pulled into a smirk.

We had emailed each other before my visit, after I had scoured the internet for experts who might explain why and for what exactly Natalie had sought help. Of course, everybody was using Post Traumatic Stress Disorder to tag a variety of afflictions, as though saying PTSD in response to nightmares and inexplicable violence, to bouts of depression and paralysis, could somehow make them less severe or offer us new insights. But PTSD was a dead end, and since I lacked the clinical terminology to describe Natalie's symptoms — if they even were symptoms — I often felt lost and overwhelmed. Yet at some point in my search, late at night and on my third or fourth drink, I came across an older article by Aloisio, and the detailed descriptions of his patients' torments had convinced me that he might be able to shed light on Natalie's condition. To a first email he never responded, but after sending a brief account of how Natalie had been found, he replied with a host of questions, and in the course of our correspondence I had provided him with more details about her disappearance and death. However, I hadn't mentioned my trips to England and Florida. Now that I was attempting to give him a fuller account of Natalie's death, I made a terrible mess of the facts, going back and forth in time, and missing important details. I sounded like an excited ten-year old. All the while, the professor's face didn't move, didn't let on whether he believed my story or found it to be utterly ridiculous.

After I had ended my jumbled report, he started to ask questions about the fire, the aftermath, about Natalie's behavior. He asked about Sonia. When I brought up Farid's and Kurt's cases, he inquired about the timelines and about the circumstances of their deaths. His plump fingers tapped out short rhythmic bursts on his knees.

"I've never heard about Kusôzu, but it's an interesting facet. I rather like it, you know. You have to admire someone's ability to externalize internal processes and to find just the right image or ritual." He abruptly stopped, apologizing for his language. "I can't help but get excited. In a strange way — I mean, not in real life, of course, but from an abstract point of view — this is quite beautiful."

"This is real life," I reminded him.

"And I do sincerely apologize. I'm glad you found me, which is, in and of itself, a bit unusual these days. My colleagues are not happy with my work, and they do try to shun me as best they can. Ever heard of Morgellons disease?"

I shook my head. Aloisio spoke with a lisp that seemed to dissipate whenever I tried to make sure I had heard correctly. Just like his smirk, you clearly noticed it until you tried to pin it down.

"Morgellons disease splits the medical profession," he continued. "Few truly believe in it, but those who do are being ostracized. It's a condition characterized by a belief that parasites or fibers are emerging from the skin. People with this condition often feel as if something is crawling on or stinging their skin. The itching and the sores can drive people crazy. I like to call it tinnitus of the skin. Some doctors believe the condition to be delusional infestation and prescribe antidepressants and antipsychotic drugs. Counseling too. A few think that the symptoms are related to an infectious process in skin cells.

"I haven't made up my mind about Morgellons, so why am I telling you about this? Because I came up with a theory several years ago. I used to work with trauma patients, but some of their behaviors I couldn't explain. Something just didn't make sense to me. And what these patients told me also didn't fit the normal categories. All the treatments we knew, all the counseling, didn't really show any effects.

"In response to what I saw, I suggested that what my patients had suffered was a 'seamless split.' I regret that term by now, I should have used something less provocative, something more abstract-sounding. But I liked the 'seamless split.' Though nowadays, should you google the term, you'll get directed to seamless split-neck bralettes and seamless split-neck crops." Dr. Aloisio grinned with such obvious satisfaction that I got up from my seat.

"I shouldn't have come," I said.

"I'm terribly sorry," he said. "Please sit down again. I do get carried away."

I did as he had told me. I had come for help, and at least he was willing to see me. "So, what you're saying is that Natalie had split personality disorder?" I asked.

"Dissociative Identity Disorder, we call it now. In the past, it was known as multiple personality disorder. People with DID have two or more distinct personalities. They're not simple changes in traits or moods. A person with DID expresses significant differences between these alternate identities, which can also be referred to as alters. Often, these personalities are completely different from each other. These fragmented personalities take control of the person's identity. But people also maintain their primary or host identity, which is their original personality, and will answer to their given name. Their primary identity is generally more passive, and they may be unaware of the other personalities."

"Unaware? They don't know when they switch?"

"Correct. When a personality change happens, the new personality will have a distinct history, a new identity, and different behaviors. And it gets stranger still. These split personalities, or alters, often have their own distinct name, age, gender, moods, memories, and vocabulary. A new personality will see themselves differently. For instance, someone assigned male at birth may have an alternate identity as a woman. They may experience themselves with female biological sex characteristics. The shift between these personalities tends to occur when a person faces a certain stressor or trigger. The exact cause of DID is not fully understood, but it's safe to assume that in the majority of cases there is a strong link between the condition and trauma. Many patients experience frequent gaps in memory and personal history, which are not due to normal forgetfulness, including forgetting everyday events."

"That wasn't the case with Natalie. Not at all."

Aloisio nodded. "No, what you describe is very different. If I follow correctly, your wife changed after the fires, as evidenced by her secret storage rooms and the paper house. But she never forgot who she was. Natalie didn't produce an Isaiah or an Elizabeth. She maintained her name, age, sex, and so forth."

I nodded. "It would have been strange if the fires hadn't changed us at all."

Aloisio kept watching me long after I had finished my remark. I couldn't tell whether he was thinking about that response or merely not paying attention anymore.

"What I observed in some patients," he said at last, "is a split more complete than DID, but it's much harder to detect. It's as if the person who experienced the trauma remains behind in time and, sometimes, in place. Someone else, someone who bears the same name and shares a personal history, continues."

"Like a body snatcher?"

Aloisio cocked his head. "Not quite. They both remain, but only one is visible. They are like twins, but only one leaves the house and is fully active. The other is, so to speak, dormant, and the one who is continuing life after the traumatic event does nothing to awaken that original self. It's not malice. Just like a DID patient, this visible self might not know it left someone else behind. They might feel at times disoriented or lost, empty even, but they don't doubt that their identity is true."

He got up to brew some coffee, pouring water from a large thermos into the small coffee maker on his desk. "Will you have some?" he asked.

"Yes," I said. "This sounds, I don't know, it sounds a bit..."

"Hokey?" he offered. "That's what my colleagues think. Too fairy-tale-ish, perhaps too unsettling. But really, if you take some time and think about it, it's far less outlandish than what we know to be true about how our minds work. In this case, a person comes to an insurmountable hurdle, our traumatic event. They cannot continue, and to stay alive, another person, one that looks like them and mostly acts like them, is created and continues." Aloisio got up, his remarkable gut tight like a large nut. He took two mugs from a bookshelf and poured the very black coffee, then sank back onto his chair with a sigh.

"Is the split seamless only for friends and family? Or do these people slowly become aware of the fact that there are two of them?"

He considered my question for the few moments it took me to burn my tongue on the scalding liquid. He must have watched me, because he said, "I should have warned you. I always use hot water to make my coffee. My little machine here is too weak to get it to the right temperature." He stopped briefly; maybe he had lost his thread. "As I said earlier, I don't believe that patients are initially aware of what they're going through, much like our DID patients don't realize they are inhabiting or performing different personalities. But some might realize that their lives have lost a certain vibrancy, and once they observe this, they start to question what they are doing. I think that's when you see marriages breaking apart, patients changing jobs and careers, or engaging in risky behaviors. They become aware of their limitations, and they want to experience just how much they have been missing. The risk of suicide is not insubstantial, but people affected by the split wouldn't describe it as that, I believe. They might say, 'I'm going home,' or 'I want to go back to the way I felt in the past.' You could say that suicide is the ultimate dare."

"You have treated people who experienced this 'seamless split.' Am I right?"

Aloisio nodded. "I've tried."

"No success?"

He cocked his head again, as though he hadn't quite understood, or maybe my question had insulted him. But his voice, when he finally answered, was as lispy and calm as before. "Most patients seemed to improve once they started their sessions with me. But the progress wasn't permanent, and many reacted with extreme anger or started to get more depressive. Three of my patients took their own lives, which is why I was dubbed 'the suicide shrink.' I still carry that moniker, even though I haven't seen patients for years. I'm teaching now, as you can see, and I'm not mentioning the seamless split anymore. It's curious you found me at all, though of course, the internet can be forever. I'm leading a quiet life these days."

There was a question somewhere buried in my mind, but even after I had emptied my mug of bad coffee, I couldn't gain access to that question. I thanked Aloisio and shook his soft hand. I found a bathroom and washed my face, staring stupidly into the mirror as though the visit to the suicide shrink could have altered my features. But no, it was still just me, slightly overweight and balding. It was just me, and there was little solace in that.

Once I was back outside, I got quickly lost once more, and worse, I couldn't find my car. I walked from building to building but couldn't remember a single one. I couldn't recall how I had gotten here, and the students, patients, and staff populating every walkway and plaza frightened me. When in the end I stood in front of my Mitsubishi, I seemed to have lost my keys. I rummaged through my pockets and my bag again and again, until I found them stuck in the ignition. It took long minutes to stop the shaking of my hands.

7

In the coming days, I often asked myself if I shared Natalie's affliction. Was I an impostor in my own life? If the doctor had indeed been right, how was I to find out? Yes, my life looked less vibrant than it once had, but wasn't that to be expected after fifty years on this dying planet? After losing Natalie twice, how could I expect to feel any different? And still, before going to bed at night, and after getting up in the morning to feed my dogs, I often wondered if I had left another man behind. Was that other Gray Harden still living in the old house, stuck forever in a life that couldn't possibly continue? And the question I hadn't been able to ask Dr. Aloisio wormed itself back into my mind, day after day. Had any patient of his ever reconnected with the person they had abandoned? Did he think those who had killed themselves had achieved that feat?

*

Since I hadn't produced new work in weeks, I canceled the lease for my gallery and, after searching for new accommodations for me, Tonda, and Anemone, moved into a small cottage near Bodega. The dogs loved the change — an acre of fenced-in land surrounded the building. Because it had no direct access to Wi-Fi and only 450 square feet of living space, the owner let me rent it for a reasonable price. I felt I wasn't going to stay for long, but in the absence of any more concrete plans, I didn't want to leave the area.

I went back to picking up trash north of Bodega Bay. I made it a habit of getting up long before sunrise so I had the beach to myself, and Tonda and Anemone could chase each other unhindered by leashes. I picked up toys toddlers and their parents had left behind, half-buried in ruined sandcastles or caught in seaweed, and put them in my backpack. Sinkers and small traps I collected as well, washing them in the kitchen sink of my new home and hanging them on the walls in the small living area and tiny bedroom. After a beach outing, the dogs might stay indoors for an hour or two, but on most days, they refused to join me inside until nightfall.

Even though I attempted it repeatedly, filling a canvas with anything but the paper house proved impossible. As hard as I might try, my mind refused to let go of Natalie's work. I tried not to let it bother me, but I grew more and more morose. It felt as though I had lost control over my hands. At night I often dreamed of the small book, and sometimes Nathan and I would sit together at a table, the book opened to a certain chapter. Other nights, Mrs. Sadeghi joined us and read aloud from the slightly yellowed pages. Each morning, I woke with a sense of dread. I was certain that something drastic needed to happen, but though I felt worse every day, I held on to the conviction that any step I might take to force the issue would only lead me astray.

I shouldn't have worried. Near the end of May I received her letter. I can't describe exactly what had made me believe I would hear from Ursa Carmel again. Call it vanity — whoever this person was, they had to be afraid I might stumble about their identity and whereabouts. Or maybe I just felt that too many loose ends had been left behind; somebody would have to come and take care of them. Beth, the break-in, the previous letter, weren't they proof that someone wanted me to be quiet and stop digging around? I'd expected this letter to arrive at an earlier date, but I'd never doubted I would be contacted again.

Following a brief phone call, Detective Glasgow drove out to visit me that afternoon. Fog was already moving in, and the wind had grown more insistent. In West County, the wind was a jealous lover, always grabbing you, never leaving you alone. It mussed your hair, put its cold hands inside your coat and under your sweater to reach for your naked skin. It berated you until your face and head hurt.

"You said good-bye to the bouge life," Glasgow said after he'd entered the cottage. His fingers combed through his hair to flatten the mess the wind had made. "In Santa Rosa, it's twenty degrees warmer than here."

"It suits me," I said. "You always know you're alive."

"Has that been a problem?" he asked.

I thought of my visit to Dr. Aloisio but said nothing.

"I had given up on ever hearing from you again. You never called after coming back from Florida." Glasgow took a few steps here, a few steps there, inspecting the ocean detritus pinned to the walls. "You didn't tell me anything."

I hadn't given it much thought, but he was right. He hadn't called after sending me down to St. Petersburg, and I had failed to follow up with him once again. Something in his tone of voice, however, confirmed what I must have known all along, without ever stopping to investigate the matter. "You knew already what I would find. You knew Nathan and I looked like brothers."

Glasgow took a seat on the ratty sofa the rancher had pulled from a shipping container at the front of his property. "You've been slow to recognize the patterns."

"Was it staged, then? Staged for my benefit? Was Nathan just another actor?"

He shook his head almost imperceptibly, he wasn't one for theatrical gestures. "Nobody can stage such a thing. I merely helped you connecting the dots."

"Did you know that Kurt had acquired my painting?"

Glasgow looked at me with a half-open mouth. I explained in a few words what I had found.

"No," he finally said. "Though I can't say I'm surprised. These things have strange ripple effects."

"Something like 'great minds think alike'?"

"Nothing so obvious, but yes, we do create peculiar force fields. People want there to be an all-knowing being, some God that gives meaning to all the small things that happen to us. They want to see connections where there are none. Our search sometimes makes us blind to the things that do connect."

I scoffed at his words. "What role are you playing in all this? 'Our search makes us blind'? What are you even talking about?"

He was quiet, staring at his hands in front of him. His fingers, long and bony, were slightly crooked at the tip. He had large hands; you could tell he'd never worked with them for a paycheck. "I'll tell you a story," he finally began. "A few years back, a colleague sent me a report via email. Someone we had an eye on had disappeared from the area and been found dead near Boise, Idaho. The report was nine pages long, I remember that, and I started printing the file. But the printer stopped suddenly, and when I checked, it said that the job had been canceled. That printer had been in the department for years, and it had never interrupted a job in that way. Sure, sometimes you run out of ink or paper, but never this. My computer couldn't find the printer either. I unhooked the cables, plugged them back in. I held four correctly printed pages in my hands, the fifth one was blank.

"As soon as I was ready to print again, the earthquake hit. A 4.4, just a mile or two away from us. It was violent and sent everyone to seek cover under their desks. The aftershock was almost as violent as the initial quake. It took a while before everything calmed down again. People were upset, shaken really, if you can forgive the pun. We hadn't had one like that in a long time.

"Finally I was ready to print the remaining pages. Once I'd read halfway through the document, I left for the day. Up and left. Didn't tell anyone I was leaving." He looked up from his hands once more. "On page five, the page the printer hadn't been able to print before the quake, the report detailed how our suspect had been found in the rubble of an old factory he'd been squatting in. He had died in his sleep. A mild earthquake had caused the abandoned building to cave."

I didn't know whether I should laugh or yell at him. "Are you saying that the universe wanted to warn you? That God or some higher power wanted to let only you know about the danger of an earthquake? Nobody else was important enough to receive a message, but you were?"

He sucked in his lips, leaving only a thin slit sitting in his face. Then he rubbed his nose, cheeks, and chin until he looked like himself again. "If you stare at the sublime a bit too long it might seem ridiculous in the end. No, it wasn't a sign. Nor was it a warning. Neither was it mere coincidence. I don't know what it was, but it happened. It was a connection. We are not trained to make sense of these. Like the sounds Nathan must have told you about. They are so loud that we can't hear them. He sees connections, but whatever web they create escapes him."

Something in the way he said this gave me pause. It wasn't the tone of his voice, nor was it the mention of Nathan. "You know of the book. *The Nine Thoughts.* Were you the person who gave it to Natalie?"

Glasgow stared at me, his face not giving away any thoughts. "You're still combing through the small stuff." He waved at the sinkers and traps and toy shovels on the walls. "You're still looking for things you can cling to. You sift through detritus and look for small, shiny objects. You look for riches when you know you've lost everything."

"Lost everything," I repeated stupidly.

"You keep up the old routine, pretending you are still the same. You keep insisting that someone murdered your wife, because if you find the guilty party, you don't have to ask who you have become."

I walked into the tiny kitchen and opened the cabinet. I took the bottle to where Glasgow sat, filled one tumbler for him and a second one for myself. I drank quickly; he didn't touch his glass. "So, who have I become then, Detective? And where is the old Gray Harden? Have I buried him? Would you like a shovel to dig him up? Is he buried under the caved-in roof of some abandoned factory? Will you send cops to plow my land and search for his body?"

He leaned back for a moment, closing his eyes, exhaling slowly. "You've got it all wrong, but I'm not the right person to tell you what you need to know."

"Did you meet Natalie at the hotel pool? Did you invite her to your room?"

He got up and moved toward the door. "You don't like looking at yourself, even though you pride yourself on your mind. You had fun traveling around the country hiding from what was in front of you."

*

It was June 6th when I boarded the plane to Seattle. In the letter, I had been given a day and a promise that someone would contact me after my arrival. My landlord in Bodega would take care of Tonda and Anemone.

The house I rented for a week stood on a hill overlooking the water. That first night, after coming back from a brief shopping trip to the nearest grocery store, I sat on the deck drinking bourbon, eating a pre-made prosciutto sandwich. On the small table in front of me lay the photo Sonia had sent me before killing herself. Natalie's solemn face — I had interpreted it as showing fear, resolve, calm, depending on when I looked at the picture. Each time, I now concluded, I had used her face as a mirror for my own feelings. What she had felt while Sonia had fidgeted with the camera I would never know.

I stayed up late, taking a walk down to the waterfront, then found myself in a half-empty bar ordering an Old Fashioned. The bartender left me alone, the other patrons seemed not to notice my arrival. When I looked up from my second drink, I saw a face reflected in the mirror behind the bar and turned around. I quickly paid and ran outside, right up to the window through which Beth had been looking at me. But there was no one in the street. I couldn't hear the sound of footsteps growing fainter. Only an old diesel truck lumbered past, the driver a guy in a cap wearing sunglasses despite the late hour.

*

The voice on the other end could have belonged to a man or a woman. It asked me to listen closely, then proceeded to read a list of instructions. Finally, it announced that the list would be send to me by email. "If you fail to show in time for the meeting, this will have been our last communication."

"Beth?" I asked.

The line went dead, and seconds later the promised message arrived in my inbox.

I squandered that day, tired and restless as I was. I sat in a coffee shop for a while, but when a woman asked if she could join me, I barked something rude and left. I strolled through the library, a building I had long wished to visit, I joined tourists at the Pike Place Market, had a glass of wine at the bar of a nearly empty restaurant. Later, at the rented house, I drank myself to sleep, only to wake up three hours later, with a dry mouth and a headache.

At three in the morning, I walked downstairs, locked the front door, and got into the car. I had rented the place for another four days, but it seemed doubtful I would ever come this way again. There might not be enough left of me to make the return trip.

I arrived in Anacortes an hour before the six o'clock ferry's departure, as the voice on the phone had instructed me to. A space had been booked for me, and I paid for my ticket and spent my time near the front of the boat, watching a landscape I couldn't quite understand. I was sweating and getting cold, I swallowed more Advil. Tourists' faces disappeared behind phones and expensive cameras, pointing here and there. I gathered they found it all to be beautiful.

It's one thing to make plans that might involve your own dissolution, and another thing to follow through on them, especially at 6:30 in the morning. The love I had felt for Natalie, the urgency that had driven me to this point, they were gone. And still, after the fifty minutes it took to arrive on Orcas Island, I got behind the wheel of my car and started toward Eastsound. I had bought two coffees on the ferry, and they kept me company on the short drive north. By eight o'clock I had made a left, and a few minutes later, I arrived in West Beach, which consisted of a few houses, a resort hotel, a farm, and little else. Without difficulty, I located the dock near the resort the voice had described to me. They would find me, the voice had said, and after that there had been no more descriptions.

Maybe ten or twelve boats had been tied to the dock. Was somebody keeping an eye on me from behind the blind window of a boat, making sure I'd come alone? I hadn't informed Glasgow of my itinerary, yet I imagined he was keeping track of my comings and goings. This was vanity perhaps, but after the Florida episode, after meeting Nathan and seeing my own painting of Natalie in Kurt's room, I couldn't be certain of anything but this: he wouldn't lift a finger to come to my rescue.

I'd never been to that part of the world. If Natalie and I had made this trip a few years earlier, maybe before our house burned down, or perhaps during the time of the rebuild when things were hectic and needed our attention and life seemed precarious and engaging, we would have thought the landscape exquisite, if maybe a tad boring. The coastline formed a shallow cove protecting the dock from the impact of storms, I imagined. At present, the waters struck me as shallow and unimpressive. Only the smell gave the ocean away. But I've always felt excluded from wooded coastlines, and after an hour of taking in my surroundings, I loathed the place. Mostly, though, I hated myself for coming.

Around ten, after I had finished the second coffee and my third protein bar, a boat appeared seemingly out of nowhere. Maybe I hadn't paid attention, or maybe it had entered the cove from the north. An old man steered the simple outboarder and, once he had come close enough to where I sat, gestured for me to climb aboard.

I nearly capsized the boat, but the man didn't make a noise, just grabbed me roughly, and pulled me down before I could fall overboard. Then we were on our way.

After the first few minutes I asked the old man where we were going. When he didn't answer, I asked again, finally touching his shoulder and repeating my question a third time. He shook off my hand and pointed to his ears; then he opened his lips wide. I had never seen a mouth missing its tongue before. I stumbled back, sat down again, and just watched Waldron Island grow bigger in front of us. To the north, a container ship was headed for Vancouver.

It was a nearly straight line to Mail Bay, but when I could already make out a small dock and a few structures beyond, we headed north, and a few minutes later, the old man jumped from the boat and pulled it onto a pebble beach. Once I stood next to him, he pointed to what looked to be a road. A strange grunting sound escaped his lips, and when I didn't move immediately, he gave me a shove. Before I had reached the graveled path, he had pushed off again.

A truck that had seen better days and was missing a headlight stood under a tree. The windows had been rolled down, or else, were broken. "Gas is pretty scarce here." A woman got out to greet me. She was perhaps my age, burly, with short hair and a wide face. "We don't have much use for these." She kicked the rusty bumper, took my bag and heaved it into the bed. "It's just a short drive."

"Is this where Ursa Carmel lives?" I asked after getting in and pulling the rusty and creaky door shut.

"Who is that?" The woman smiled at me as though I had made a funny remark she didn't quite follow. "Did you have a good trip?"

"Who lives here?" I pointed at a few houses to our right.

"It's about a hundred of us. Twice that many in the summer. We don't have electricity or water services, so we're a pretty exclusive club."

"Generators?" I asked.

She smiled again. Maybe it was me who wasn't in on her joke. "And solar panels. As I said, it's hard to get fuel on Waldron. And we like it that way. Keeps the summer people to a minimum."

The gravel road turned away from the water, and the woman slowed down to navigate some potholes. Nothing but trees wherever I looked. "It's ideal to make someone disappear."

"Say what?" Again this wide smile that tugged at her eyes until they were reduced to mere slits. "I'm Maggie, by the way. Aaron asked me to pick you up."

"Aaron?"

"He drives the ambulance whenever we need it. We don't need it a lot. He twisted his ankle, his right one, so he asked me to get you."

"And where are you taking me?"

"You don't know?" She laughed, revealing very white, very regular teeth. "What kind of traveler are you?"

I shrugged. "The one with lots of questions."

She shook her head at that, or maybe it was just another pothole that made her head bob.

After another two or three minutes, Maggie stopped and turned to me. "This is it."

I looked around, but the only indication that we had arrived at a specific point was a narrow path to our right. "This way?" I pointed down the path.

"I guess," she answered. "They don't come much anymore. Don't pay anyone to keep it up either."

I thanked her, got out, grabbed my bag, which had slid over to the other side of the truck, then waited until Maggie had disappeared around a bend. The smell of oil hung in the air for several minutes after. From afar I meant to hear the horn of a ship. Other than that, I couldn't hear a thing.

The path was strewn with old needles, smaller and larger branches. If someone had come this way before me, they hadn't left any trace. A doe with two fawns tore me from my useless thoughts, thoughts and conjured images I hadn't even noticed and that I immediately forgot. The three stared at me, and I stared at them, unmoving. Then suddenly, reacting to something I couldn't hear or see, they took off noiselessly down the path, and I followed.

The shutters had been taken down and piled up near the entrance of the house. It was made entirely from wood and had never been painted, the surfaces looking as gray as stone, moss covering much of the roof. The entrance door, when I tried, opened with a low creak. Several windows stood open, but even so, the interior smelled of rotten food, a smell that stung like smoke.

The house only had three rooms. A small bathroom in the far corner with sink and toilet; a bedroom with two bunkbeds; and the main room, which held a sofa and two armchairs on one side and a spartan kitchen with a wood cook stove at its center on the other. A dining table with six chairs divided the halves.

I dropped my bag on the table, ate a fourth protein bar while looking through the cabinets. I found the usual assortment of ugly plates and mismatched coffee cups, silverware that had never been fancy, and pans that seemed to have been in use since the gold rush. But behind one door I found a few bags of pasta, canned fish and meat, sauce, a loaf of bread, jam, and several bars of chocolate.

The first and second gallons of water looked and smelled like sewage, but after that I was able to fill an old pot and put it on the stove. Wood I found outside, neatly stacked by the side of the house, and I collected dry branches and lit them with matches that looked ancient but had been kept dry. The house filled with smoke immediately, but once the logs caught fire, I was able to enter the house once more. The coughing soon subsided. Somewhere, I thought, someone is standing behind a tree keeping watch. They are laughing, watching this hapless man trying to make his first meal on Waldron. What fun I must be to watch. What joy.

What my hosts had forgotten was salt, and even my third try of finding some leftover container in the house brought up nothing. The pasta, morosely overcooked, tasted like the skin you bite off your fingers dipped in marinara sauce. My stomach calmed down, though. I gnawed on the bread, dug into some canned trout, and by three o'clock I was asleep in one of the bunks. I left the door unlocked. I felt certain I wouldn't be alone for long.

My watch glowed too dimly for me to read the time when I awoke. I was sweaty, I remember that, sweaty and cold. My feet fished for the shoes I had taken off before lying down.

"Took you a while," the voice said from the main room. "I'm glad you're awake."

No light came from the room, at least nothing you could call that. The windows, only shielded by threadbare curtains, glowed faintly, but they didn't help me locate my visitor. I stepped from the bedroom unsure where to turn.

"Sit down in the kitchen. Don't try anything funny. I'm holding a taser and I know how to use it."

I bumped my knee into the table, pulled a chair, and sank down. I thought I could see a person's silhouette on the sofa, but in my state, anything would have looked like the silhouette of a person. "How many of you are here?"

"Just me. I'm the one you want to talk to."

"You are? How would I know?"

"You'll find out soon enough. For now, let's talk." There was something odd about the voice. It was clear enough, and yet I couldn't decide whether it belonged to a man or a woman. It sounded too deep and raw to be a woman's voice, and yet too circumspect to be a man's. But no, that doesn't describe it at all. The voice sounded as though both a man and woman were talking at the same time, two separate people.

"You're Ursa Carmel," I said.

"I'm the person you've been following."

My fingers slowly, silently searched the table for the box of matches. "Will I disappear like my wife? Will I lose my feet? Will I turn up in a hotel room covered in paint? Will I look decomposed?"

"I think you might know that already."

"Why are we sitting in the dark?" I asked. "Why didn't you show yourself back in California? You were in my house. Why didn't you come then? Why did I have to travel to this island to speak to you?" My fingers hit the empty fish can, but I thought the sound was only audible to me.

The voice didn't speak until some twenty or thirty seconds later. "People who seek me out often die, but I'm no killer. I arrive when people need me, I don't show up to scare them."

My hand closed around the matchbox, and slowly I pushed it open. "Did you bring the salt?"

"Don't do that," the voice said. "You'll see me soon enough."

"Are you that ugly?"

"You're not ready yet. Now close your eyes."

To my surprise, that's exactly what I did, and I didn't open them until much later, until I was certain that the room was empty once again and that whoever had paid me a visit was beyond my grasp.

<h1 style="text-align:center">8</h1>

It's odd how sometimes your reaction to an event or something you observe, fails to match up. Weddings and birthday parties have always made me feel gloomy, whereas TV shows about fictional serial killers have often left me giddy. And even stranger are the short-term and long-term effects of one's actions.

In my thirties, I took up running. Soon I started to participate in road races. Each event left me exhilarated. For hours after a race, I felt at peace, strangely satisfied with the world and my place in it. But toward evening, I would start to question the value of such an activity. The world, I felt, had no need for me. I was an outcast and would remain one forever.

I had a good friend once, a teacher of mine who suddenly, years after my graduation, turned into a confidante and a mentor. After every meeting with her, and later after every phone call, I became angry or morose. Her confidence, her love for me, her contentedness and her humor warmed me, but an hour or so later, once I was alone again, I felt terrible about myself. I felt an irrational anger toward her brashness. Who was she to give me advice? Yet the next morning, something seemed to have cleared, each and every time. I felt energized, I no longer harbored anger toward her. It felt like I had taken an important hurdle.

If that sounds vague, it's because it is. I couldn't explain my reactions then, and I can't now, but when the glow of the windows intensified, and I could once again make out the chairs, the stove, and the sofa, I was happy that I had come. I was eager to see Ursa Carmel again. I took a sponge bath with cold water and some dish soap, put on new clothes, then sat on the stoop drinking coffee, listening to the island awaken around me. I wasn't part of it, I didn't belong; just being there felt like enough.

*

The airfield came into view ten minutes into my walk. For a few moments I had hesitated to leave the house, then decided that I would be found no matter where on Waldron I might be. No instructions had been given to me, and I felt that the person who had sat across from me in the dark had no use for calendars, appointment books, or a strict schedule. The high I had felt in the early morning hours hadn't faded. I was convinced that I couldn't miss her. She would be there whenever she wanted to see me.

I followed the grassy lane north, then entered the forest once more. Soon, I arrived at Severson Bay. The islands to the west barely rose above the horizon; a coast guard ship was heading out this side of the Canadian border. I sat down on a bleached log but found I was too excited to stare into the distance. Instead, I walked along the gravelly beach until I turned south again, certain I would find my house without a problem.

I had just finished another saltless meal when Maggie's truck stopped outside; this time she had braved the narrow path. Yet it wasn't Maggie who stepped out and walked toward the house. I moved away from the window as if to hide but didn't get far — there was no hidden room, no dark corner for me to disappear into. And after she entered, it took Beth only one glance to spot me; something akin to a smile appeared on her lips and disappeared just as quickly. I might not have worn a look she recognized.

"Did you bring some salt with you?" I said. "The food on this island has been very bland."

The smile reappeared. "I don't think we have time to prepare a meal together."

She wore tight jeans and a loose-fitting fishtail parka over a thin woolen shirt. She looked gaunter than I remembered, her teeth in that smile longer, glassier. The lines around her eyes appeared deeper, though that might have been the antics of the afternoon light.

"She wants to talk to me."

Beth shook her head. "It's not what you think. I have a favor to ask of you."

"Do I owe you one?" I was still standing near the window, hadn't moved since she had opened the front door. I wanted to walk up to her, I wanted to take her hand, but her appearance had been too sudden. My wish to feel her fingers only paralyzed me. I was vindictive.

"It would be nice not to have to go alone."

"Where to?"

Age is a weird thing. I was fifty now, old enough to have grandkids had I chosen that path, but I remained at the window like a mere child waiting to be released and for its anger to be seen and mollified. I'm ashamed of my reaction, or better, the lack thereof. My face is growing hot as I recall this episode, and I shake my head as though I could make the scene of that afternoon disappear. It's futile. A second later, I see Beth walk around the dining table toward where I stand with clenched jaw. She reaches for my hands and joins them behind her back. "I could use your presence. I'm not supposed to come alone."

Our teeth clicked against one another, so pathetic were our attempts at a kiss. Her hands were icy, but I didn't squirm. I thought of Natalie, who I had betrayed so badly, yet not even my wife's memory stopped my hands from exploring Beth's skin, her neck, her head, her hips. My hands seemed too small to ever get a hold of her.

It wasn't pretty. It was over before it had really begun. Or that's how I felt. What it was to her, I shudder to contemplate. "Come on, people are waiting," she whispered in my ear. I couldn't imagine what use I could be to her. But if these were the last moments of my life, I wanted to feel them, each and every single one.

Afterward, we looked unchanged, disappointingly so. We hadn't been transformed by the experience, and not even her coat looked rumpled or torn. When I grabbed my bag on the way out, she shook her head. "You won't need this."

"Who will clean up and make it disappear? You?"

She stopped in the door, and I had never seen anyone look so disenchanted and miserable. That look has stayed with me and poisons the memory of what happened before my question, the few short moments when the sauce-splattered plates crashed to the floor and broke, and a fork dug into my arm. "It's not about you." She wasn't upset, just stating her point.

"But I'm going to die here," I said. "This is the deal. I get to see Ursa Carmel the healer, killer, whatever she thinks she is, and I have to pay the price."

Beth shook her head, the odd look on her face remained in place. "Please," she said. "Please."

*

The drive took us to the western side of the island and was predictably short. Beth parked the truck at the end of a dirt road, and in time we followed a narrow path down to the beach. The water seemed so quiet, it felt as though we were looking out onto a deep lake. "Will you take a photo of us?" she asked.

I took my phone from the coat pocket, and another image came to mind. Sonia and Natalie, standing on another beach, a masked figure behind them. I turned to scan the beach for an intruder, but we remained the only visitors.

"Did you get the two of us?"

I nodded. "Wanna see?"

"As long as we're both in that picture, it's all good. Let's walk."

"Where are we going?" I tried to hand her the phone, but she refused. "You take it," I said. "I don't want them to have it."

She shook her head, smiled to erase the look of displeasure. Then she took my hand and led me north. "You still don't understand," she said.

"I don't think I was ever given enough time. You always seem to disappear before I can ask the right questions."

She seemed to think about that, gripped my hand tighter. "I used to live outside of Los Angeles, toward San Bernardino. My husband taught at a college, a very posh, private one. Our house was small, and we could barely afford it, but we managed. In 2016, we had to evacuate because of a wildfire."

"I'm sorry," I said. "You lost your home."

She glanced at me before turning her head back toward the water. "We didn't. Our neighborhood was spared. We'd gotten away with a scare. Friends of ours had lost everything, but we only had some smoke damage. We were lucky. Then the following spring we experienced heavier-than-usual rains. On the third day, while my husband was at work, I made a quick run to the grocery store; I was working from home editing school books. The milk had gone sour and I wanted more coffee. Leaving the house during this weather felt silly, you know that Southern Californians can't drive in the rain. They make the stupidest mistakes. I was maybe halfway down our block when I saw two people by the side of the road wildly gesturing and I looked into the rearview mirror just in time to see the houses behind me being pushed off their foundations and into the street before collapsing and disappearing. Half a block just slid off the hill, and the debris buried other houses farther down the slope. We weren't even allowed to dig through the mud, not that it would have helped. The national guard came in and helped with the clean-up."

"Did you rebuild?"

"I was pregnant with our first child. We moved into a hotel for the first two weeks and then found some apartment twenty minutes away. One night, Alex didn't come home. When I tried to reach him at work, they said that he had quit his job. I've never quite understood that reaction. Maybe because his life had been washed away, he noticed that he hadn't wanted it in the first place. You know, maybe the escape from the fire had made him understand that his time with me had come to an end. But it's hard to extract yourself when you share a mortgage, share a routine, share what seems to be a somewhat predictable future. Steadiness is a good substitute for love. In any case, when we had nothing left, he disappeared.

"I miscarried. It wasn't my husband's fault. I was careful, but it happened anyway. I moved to New Mexico, found another job, and after two years bought a condo. I had a new life."

"But it didn't mean anything."

"I'm not in it. I can't feel it. I'm here but really, I'm still standing in front of the barricades the national guard erected, staring up at the place where our house had disappeared. I've never moved away from there."

"Why didn't you tell me back in Reno?"

"I had a different role to play. It wasn't my story that was playing out."

"But how is this your story now? I'm meeting Ursa Carmel, and I don't expect to make it off this island. Maybe she'll tell me what I've come to find out. Maybe she'll let me know why she needed to kill Natalie."

Beth stopped and turned to me, framing my face with her hands. "You're not here for your wife, Gray. That's not how it works. You are here for me. I chose you."

"You chose me? For what?"

"I want you to be my second. I want you to be there."

"Where? Where do you want me to be?"

She let go of me, nodded her head toward a house that stood a quarter mile up the beach, still half hidden by trees.

"Is she going to be there? Why didn't you drive us there?"

"They need to see us. They need to see we're alone. They need to see we're coming without haste. They need to see we're willing to see them."

I shook my head. "Did you meet Natalie? Were you...?" I stopped, my mind racing, trying to catch up with Beth. "Why did you tell me that I was a shit and didn't deserve Natalie? Why did you tell me that? Why are you asking me to be your 'second?'"

"You're stronger than your wife was. No, not stronger, just...you can't get lost the way she did. That's something you can be grateful for." She paused for a brief moment. "We have to go now." And with that, she walked toward the house she had pointed out, letting go of my hand before we reached the weather-beaten structure.

We had come within thirty feet of the entrance when the door opened and a woman stepped onto the porch. She wore a somewhat shapeless dress in purple and different shades of green, and an unbuttoned cardigan in rust-red over that. Her boots were of a mustard yellow. She took a few steps toward us, and a smile spread on her face. "I'll steal her from you, if you allow," she said brightly, and I knew it was this woman who had visited me the night before. She wasn't tall, nor was her appearance imposing in any physical way, but as soon as she spoke, Beth and I seemed to shrink, in size, will, and importance. Again, I had the feeling that two people were speaking at the same time to me, yet even though I grew angry at her words, the sound of her voice was soothing, invigorating even. No matter how much I searched for the right reply, I couldn't manage to say a thing.

The woman took Beth's arm and led her up the porch; I watched them disappear into the house without interfering. How long I stood there, I can't say, but I hadn't moved an inch before the woman's figure became visible again. "You too," she said. "You're her second. I know you're trying to understand."

The inside of the house felt shabbily comfortable. Bookshelves lined two walls, the smell of spices or aromatic oils hung about, and knickknacks had infested every available surface. Gemstones, small figurines, antique appliances. In those first moments when I was alone in the living area, it felt as though I had come for a tea party and soon a tray of cucumber finger sandwiches might be carried in from the kitchen. "Make yourself comfortable." The woman had stepped through a door.

"What will I be waiting for? For her to die?"

"She won't, she won't die. You came to save her, no? You came to see me? You came to understand why your wife left you. You came to see, didn't you? You came to hear. You came to listen." The odd voice was teasing me as though I were a five-year-old. "Well, now you can save everybody. Now you can listen." With that, she left the room once more, closing the door behind her.

When I think back on that moment, it appears that it took me a very long time to try and follow the woman in the purple and green dress. My steps seem wobbly, as though I have just awakened, still too tired to coordinate my limbs. It should only take a second to reach the door, but many minutes pass. I see my hand reach for the doorknob as though I strain against a strong current or a strong wind. Every small motion becomes difficult. Then I see my hand close around the knob, but it won't turn. I bang against the door, panicked all of a sudden. The odd paralysis lifts all of a sudden, and I bang and shout, but nothing happens for the next few seconds. Minutes maybe. I can't remember how long I stood in front of the door and shouted, but I can still feel my voice growing hoarse; I had to cough. I meant to see shadows flitting about the room, and I suddenly grew exhausted. I meant to fight, I meant to break open the door to save Beth. The path was very clear, painfully so. Still, the shadows grew and multiplied, and I couldn't concentrate. My stomach hurt; I grew desperate. I waded through the ghostly bodies filling the room toward the entrance, toward the porch.

I never heard Ursa Carmel sing. It wasn't hearing, and yet her voice had taken hold of my body. How do I know her voice filled my lungs and head? How do I know it was her? I don't. I have no guarantee, no recording, the truth won't manifest itself. But I know what my body told me, I know it was her voice that followed me to the beach, sending its ghosts after me until I reached the water's edge. Her voice blurred my vision and drove me down and deeper. I sank below the surface to fill my ears and drown out her voice.

*

The smell of spices still hung about, and a steaming mug of coffee now sat in front of me. Thirty minutes had passed maybe since I'd walked into the water, and the room seemed unchanged, but my heart still couldn't find its rhythm. My hands trembled too much to pick up the hot liquid.

"Yes, your wife's friend was very helpful; I regret that she took her life — she was blameless. The boy's friend, despite his young age, understood that he had nothing to fear." The woman had changed into different, though equally gaudy, clothes. She wore a red dress now, half-covered by a brown drape. Her very small feet were barely covered by gold-colored sandals. "I depend on the seconds to fulfill their task. It's an act of mercy to guide people to the destination they have chosen for themselves, although people might view it as an act of barbarism." She paused briefly. "I hope you're comfortable."

I sat in an armchair wearing some odd garments, things maybe ripped off the bodies of the people who'd come to hear her voice. Corduroy pants, red woolen socks, an old blue hoodie. Nothing quite fit, but the clothes were dry. "And Kurt? Who was his second?"

"His sister accompanied him."

I scoffed. "Do you make the seconds lie to the family and the police to protect them or to protect yourself?" I still tasted salt and was fighting for breath. "Where is Beth?"

Her voice changed, grew deeper still. Again, I had the feeling that several people were with me in this room, speaking in unison. "Where she ought to be. That's the reason why she came, and it's the reason why you accompanied her."

"I want to see her."

"You will. I insist."

It's one thing to believe you are dying, it's another to push yourself to certainty. My embarrassment and shame over not having drowned kept me warmer than the strange assortment of clothes. "But why here? Why not in Santa Rosa or San Francisco? Why did you guide me to this forsaken island?" My voice, water-logged and hoarse, sought refuge in anger, that old friend of mine. Anger had always been the refuge when my own failings became too apparent. It was this anger that finally allowed me to look at the woman across from me and hold her gaze.

Carmel's features were large, set in a small face. Here eyes were heavily hooded, barely visible from where I sat, and deep lines cut up her face. And yet, I couldn't have guessed at her age. Somehow, she didn't appear to have been touched by age, despite her wrinkles, despite the graying hair, as though she could wipe away the signs of wear at any moment of her choosing. She laughed at my obvious attempt to size her up, turned her head this way and that like a model during a photo shoot.

"Yes, you want to remember everything." Then her laughter vanished, and she leaned back in her chair. "Why Waldron? When you got married to Natalie, did you believe the ceremony was the bond you needed to stay together?"

"Of course not."

"But you insisted on it. You went to Hawaii to get married, you didn't have the Justice of the Peace come to your backyard. You created a system of difficulties and hurdles for the ones you invited. And they all came, didn't they?" She paused a bit, she looked tired all of a sudden. "You wouldn't have been ready to be Beth's second if I had asked you to hold the ceremony in your backyard. You needed some convincing. This," her right flew up to meekly implicate the house, the beach, the whole island, "I did for you."

I pondered her answer, my face red, my forehead hot with sweat. "Why?"

"The world isn't controlled by the Illuminati, by four or five crazy billionaires, by the Jews, by a sex-trafficking elite. How easy it would be to point fingers. But we still need to make sense, your own mind needs to make sense even when the logical answer is that there isn't any. Your mind rejects chaos, it wants the trappings of cause and effect, with yourself as a key player in a well-organized if sometimes hard-to-understand universe. You want to see patterns, development, intricate solutions.

"Your wife realized, the moment your house burned down, that it wasn't some higher power who had picked her to suffer. There was no sense in the fire, no divine writer pointing their finger at her. She wasn't chosen, she merely suffered the consequences of our common fate, brought on by our greed, by how we understand our place in the world. She heard the sound of that world and stopped moving."

"She stopped moving?"

"It's just an image for you. It's much more complicated than that. But focus on that image. Once your house burned to the ground, Natalie stopped in her tracks, and someone who looked remarkably like her, took over. It was my task to free the trapped Natalie. But in order to accomplish that, I had to sing for the woman who had lived with you, who was lost among the living."

"You killed her."

"I freed your wife."

"Then where is she?"

"Right here. You could feel her if you wouldn't talk so much. If you listened to me, you could hear her." She paused for a moment. "But your ignorance is helpful. We all tell ourselves how precious we are. Couples think they are more attractive than they appear to others. All these myriad forms of delusion keep us sane. In that sense, and in that sense alone, you are quite fortunate."

"How can this — fake person — ask for her own death?"

"It was Natalie asking and it was Natalie who built the paper house to make herself remember, but she couldn't shake the impostor."

I looked for words, but nothing would come to me. My hands searched the air for what I needed to say in vain. In the end I could only utter her name, "Sonia."

"You won't suffer her fate. You are too...substantial. Stubborn. Thick."

"Thick."

"You know you only have to ask. All it takes is but an honest request."

Yes, yes, I knew, had probably known all along. I only had to ask her to sing, with the voices of all the people she had freed, I only had to ask her to sing her silent death. Sweat stains appeared on my chest and legs. My tongue felt stranded like a whale in the shallows, my eyes were red and dry, I could feel how dry and red they were. "I can't," I finally admitted. "I long to hear you, I do. Beth told me I couldn't get lost. What does that mean?"

She didn't hesitate for even a second. "Not much. Deem yourself lucky that the person you are is too coarse to be stopped by a fire. You can't feel the weight of the world, you're too stunted. You never quite knew who you were to begin with."

I couldn't stop laughing. Not even after she had risen from her armchair and held out her hand to me. I couldn't. Underneath all the anguish and doubt, the hurts and longings, the terror and the sadness, I discovered laughter. It had been there all along, unbeknownst to me. I shook with laughter, and try as I might, I couldn't take Ursa's hand. Only after long minutes did I grew too tired to continue laughing. My sides hurt and I was out of breath at last.

"It's time," she said.

And I nodded and took her hand at last.

*

This body that she had rejected, this simulacrum of the person she once had been, would never impersonate her again. Beth lay on a table not unlike the one I had encountered in the mortician's workspace. The paints were laid out next to it on a wooden cart.

I had never touched a dead body before, something so substantial that had once been endowed with life and now wasn't. I had carried my dead dog to the veterinarian's car, but I had never taken the time to touch and care for a body which was no longer inhabited. This took hours, and I was left alone with the woman I had called Beth until the decomposition appeared nearly real.

"This is your final responsibility." Ursa emptied and cleaned the cart's surface, then opened a waxed canvas knife roll. She handed me what I needed, demonstrated the swing that would be the most powerful. Using the weight of the knife rather than too much physical force, I raised the cleaver to chest height and held my forearm straight. You don't need to squeeze the knife, just hold it firmly as you bring it down.

9

There's a before and an after. There's a time after what you feared would destroy you has, in fact, happened, a time when you feel as though you're a ghost peeking in on the living. The body is lighter than the smoke of a cigarette, any thought lighter still. Sometimes your hand passes through your cup of coffee or the door of your car.

I didn't speak again until much later, until after the old man had ferried me back to Orcas Island and I was back at the ferry terminal, until I had bought a coffee to keep me company. After that I coughed up words like broken glass fragments, blubbering, spewing nonsense. My eyes were full of grit. No one approached me, nobody dared to ask. Not even the ticket collector was interested. In the early morning hours I was back at my rented house. I fell asleep leaning against the bathtub. I didn't want to ever lie down again.

*

A year after returning to my small cottage in West County, I met a woman, and she is now my wife. She is an artist, and tonight she's hanging four small canvases for a group show in a Santa Rosa café. Sylvie is excited, full of anticipation. I help her find the assigned spots and mount her work. She cocks her head and says, "You're so adept." She doesn't understand why I don't paint anymore, but in her mind, she must have made up a story that satisfies her curiosity. She has come to accept that I don't join her in the barn behind our house in West County, where she spends long hours on her work. She inherited money from an aunt in France; it's the reason why we don't see much of our dogs. Their world has grown to twenty acres with fences all around.

It's a comfortable life, one I'm still adjusting to. The miracle of loving someone for whom money has always been a set of keys tucked away in their coat pocket, leaves me blind and dumb. From time to time, I steal away from this new life and visit Natalie's storage units. I'm still paying for them, a fact I keep hidden from Sylvie. Maybe she would understand, but I don't want to do the work. From time to time, I just choose to sit in front of the paper house. One of these days I will sell off the furniture the woman who replaced Natalie assembled. I will put chairs, desk, dining table, and floor lamps on Craigslist. There is no reality to any of these items; even somebody as sturdy and solid as myself can feel this.

It's the paper house that feels more real than any of the years I have lived since the fire, any of the things I have touched, bought, or worn since. The house itself might have no heft, but the longing I feel is so strong, I make myself believe I can reach out and touch Natalie. When I die, maybe I will find her here.

"Why the feet?" I had asked Ursa Carmel before taking the knife from her hand.

"We don't want the impostor to catch up with her again, do we?" she said. "I can't risk that. I owe her that." Her voice was barely audible.

Sylvie is done filling out two forms for the show, hands them to an old woman at the desk in front and pulls me toward the exit. "That was weird," she says, and I can smell her sweet breath, the warmth that is emanating from her face and neck. Her long hair is held together in back by a pencil. "Now my paintings are out there, doing their thing." And I hold her for a brief moment; her body moves, her hands wander up to my face and down to my waist. As long as she prods and writhes, passersby might believe I'm responding and moving on my own accord. The artists who leave the café and walk past us might think that we are both in love and alive.

ABOUT THE AUTHOR

Stefan Kiesbye is the author of eight books of fiction, including *Your House Is on Fire, Your Children All Gone* and *But I Don't Know You*. His stories, essays, and reviews have appeared in the *Wall Street Journal*, *Publishers Weekly*, and the *Los Angeles Times,* among others. Kiesbye lives in San Francisco's North Bay and teaches creative writing and literature at Sonoma State University.